EXPOSE: JAXSON

EAGLE TACTICAL BOOK ONE

WILLOW FOX

SLOWBURN
PUBLISHING

Expose: Jaxson

Eagle Tactical Book One

Willow Fox

Published by Slow Burn Publishing

© 2021

CHAPTER ONE

ARIELLA

I ran for my life, and it was all *his* fault. Secrets had brought me over a thousand miles from home. I fled with only one thought in mind: a second chance. Starting over was my only option for survival.

I squinted through my sunglasses, shucking them to the empty passenger seat, finding it difficult to see. My vision adjusted, but the night was setting in fast as daylight fell over the horizon.

I struggled to see the narrow, snow-covered road ahead.

The streets at the bottom of the mountain had been freshly plowed and salted. The headlights on my five-speed were angled at odd intervals, casting shadows over the road covered in potholes beneath the slush.

The car jolted and bounced with my foot on the gas, splashing my scalding, stale coffee from the cup holder.

My eyes burned and welled.

"Shit!"

Tears threatened the surface, but I wouldn't cry. It wasn't the sting of blistering liquid that hurt. I'd done this to myself. I blamed him, but it was as much my fault.

Secrets surrounded my past. Benjamin Ryan had been part of those secrets, but there was more than even he knew. There were secrets I could never tell him, even as he was whisked away in handcuffs.

I packed my car with my possessions and hurried out of the state of New York. Of course, not before finding a small log cabin in the woods that I could afford in cash, sight unseen.

I also lined up a job interview at a nearby resort, but there was no guarantee of landing a position right away. My last one had ruined my life, and I couldn't even put it on my resume.

I'd have to be frugal with the few dollars left to my name, which consisted of a few ones in my wallet.

Was I bitter?

Sure as shit, but I moved on, started over, and prayed for a second chance. A fresh start is what I did, what I craved, and the only way to get that was to move.

I went back to using my maiden name: Ariella Cole. I wasn't in hiding per se. After all, I had done nothing wrong or criminal.

I couldn't say the same for him.

I didn't want to get mixed up in his illegal affairs.

I had planned on arriving at my new home before dark, but the interview had been in the afternoon at Blue Sky Resort, a ski lodge just outside of Breckenridge, Montana.

It was for a position covering other worker's shifts, everything from waitressing at the restaurant to doing housekeeping tasks and handling the ski rental equipment. I'd take whatever I could get.

The interview had seemed to go well, and they had asked to run a background check. I wasn't keen on it but I didn't have a choice, so they'd see that my ex-husband, Ben, had run up our credit. They couldn't deny me a job because of that, right?

He was serving time in federal prison for several felonies. That couldn't count against me, right?

When I'd left the resort, with my piping hot, burnt coffee, it had grown dark. The front desk attendant had given me directions since my phone died, and GPS was sketchy as to whether it worked in the mountains.

I headed for my new house, weary, tired, and worn after a lengthy interview and an even longer drive across the country. I wanted to discover my new home, climb into bed under the warm covers and sleep for a week.

The interviewer informed me they'd run my references, and I had to submit to a background check.

It sounded all good, and while I hoped the job was mine, there were no guarantees. They hadn't offered me anything yet.

I downshifted my car, but I struggled to get up the mountain.

The bald tires spun as I white-knuckled the steering wheel. The back of the vehicle fishtailed.

I downshifted again and stomped on the gas to climb the godforsaken beast of a mountain when the car slipped and slid backward downhill.

"Shit!" I screamed and stomped on the brakes hard, which only had me doing donuts as I spun and slid down the icy path of the mountain. I would have braced for impact if I had known how, but I just wanted to survive. I needed to survive.

My stomach ached with dread. My palms were sweaty, and I clung to the steering wheel, attempting to maneuver my car out of danger.

I had no control over the vehicle, like it had a mind of its own.

The car spun and smacked into a tree. The window smashed. It wasn't enough to stop the momentum from sliding down the mountain, and the back wheels skidded off the road.

By some miracle, the vehicle came to a halt. The back wheels teetered off the edge of a ravine.

The car's front appeared stable, but would it propel me downward and into oblivion if I made any sudden movements?

I glanced in the rearview mirror.

It grew darker by the minute, and I couldn't ascertain how far down the ditch went, but given the fact the entire drive up the mountain was switchbacks and dangerous, without a doubt, it was deadly.

Exhaling a soft, slow breath, I couldn't stay in the car. I needed to get help.

I hadn't seen a car on the road since I attempted to climb the damned mountain. Was there a reason for that? Did anyone live up in Breckenridge, or was I the only one crazy enough to head up there on the cusp of winter?

I probably should have traded my car in for a vehicle with all-wheel drive or a truck, but it wasn't like I could afford it.

I was strapped for cash. I spent every dime on getting to Breckenridge and paying cash for the cabin I found on one of the realtor sites online.

The place looked like a gem, backed up to a gorgeous river, and within walking distance to a few local shops in town.

This had to mean I wasn't the only one in Breckenridge, but they were smart enough not to travel at night up the mountain.

My phone was dead, and even if it had any juice left, I knew without a doubt there would be no cell service around here.

There had been no service at the bottom of the mountain. That had been when my phone still had a tiny amount of battery power.

Not that I didn't have anyone to call. My sister would expect to hear from me, but we weren't on the best speaking terms. She was pissed that I moved to

Breckenridge instead of staying in New York with her.

I couldn't stay. I had to get as far away from New York and the enemies we'd made.

I glanced behind me at my knapsack. I couldn't risk reaching for it. Not until I was out of the car.

With slow precision, I unlocked the door and eased the driver's side open. I made no sudden movements.

While I'd have preferred to stay in the confines of the car that offered shelter, it teetered on the edge of a ravine. I wasn't ready to meet death.

The car creaked and groaned as I was careful to shift my weight from one foot and then the other out from the vehicle.

The vehicle didn't launch off the cliff as I had first feared. I shivered and pulled my jacket tight.

I couldn't easily open the back door from my position. The snow was several inches thick, and I had stuffed my boots in the trunk.

There was no way I could maneuver myself to grab my warm and comfy shoes. My fancy heels would have to suffice because I wasn't going barefoot. That would be even stupider in this weather.

"Okay, I can do this," I said to myself.

There wasn't another soul on the road, and I didn't even want to consider what wild animals like bears or wolves come out at night. I hadn't the slightest idea if they were nocturnal. I hoped I didn't run into any creatures because I had nothing but my hands to protect me, and well, I may as well just lie down and play dead.

Okay, so getting my bag from the backseat wasn't as easy as I thought. I exhaled a nervous breath, my stomach in knots as I climbed back into the driver's seat, reached for my knapsack in the back, along with my purse on the passenger seat.

I didn't make any sudden movements, and I backed away from the car, shut the car door, shoved my purse into the bag, and swung it over my shoulder.

My hands shook from the cold and the adrenaline coursing through my veins. I dug into my pockets, retrieving a pair of leather driving gloves. They would have to suffice.

With daylight nearly gone, I headed for the main road of the mountain.

I kept to the center of the snow-covered path. I'd probably hear something long before I'd see anything, but I wasn't holding my breath.

The moon offered the faintest bit of light to illuminate the snow-covered road.

I had no flashlight, and the darkness of night seeped in, which reminded me there wasn't a town for miles because there were no city lights nearby.

I glanced up at the heavens, the frigid night air offering way to a sparkle of stars peppering the night sky. It would be a beautiful sight if it wasn't so cold and I didn't worry about freezing to death.

My lungs hurt from the cold. With each breath inward, a thousand knives were stabbing at my lungs.

With my jacket zipped up tight, I leaned my head down toward my coat. I needed to find shelter. With sundown, the night would only grow colder.

My hands trembled even with the warmth of my gloves. The edge of the road was difficult to see with no light. It seemed even more impossible to determine if there was any evidence of shelter.

I kept walking up the mountain. The only way I could tell I was headed in the correct direction was because the wind assaulted my face, and my footprints were evidence of where I'd been.

I could no longer see my car in the distance. The broken windows may have offered little shelter from the wind, but I could have been warmer had I stayed inside the vehicle. I could also have been catapulted down the ravine had I so much as shifted the car's weight.

There was no use second-guessing my decision. I just hoped that the main road would lead off to a driveway, a house, a cabin, or some sign of civilization.

The chill of the cold brought tears to my eyes, freezing my eyelashes, stinging my cheeks. My hands were numb, and my knapsack offered no clothes. Frozen inside and out.

I stumbled over my feet.

My toes burned from the frigid air that assaulted every inch of my body. The sensation went beyond numb and tingling.

I tripped and braced myself as I hit hard-packed snow on the road, eating a mouthful. I spit out the contents as best I could.

My lips were numb, along with my cheeks.

I shivered and curled up in the fetal position in the middle of the snow-covered road. I buried my face away from the chill.

Shielding my cheeks from the cold, getting an ounce of warmth and a reprieve from the elements. I pulled my bag closer to protect me from the wind. I shut my eyes.

My body trembled, but I wasn't cold. Not like I had been earlier. Numb. Nothing but emptiness, a cold and lonely existence stabbing at me.

CHAPTER TWO

JAXSON

I turned the satellite radio up. It was the only channels that came in within a hundred miles of Breckenridge.

We were literally in the middle of nowhere. Just the way I liked it. I've lived in Montana all my life, grew up in a small town a few hours from Breckenridge.

I cranked the music, letting it blare and taking a few minutes to myself after a long day visiting the next town over, I drove the main pass through Breckenridge.

It was late. The road was not well-traveled, let alone between storms. While it wasn't currently snowing, there were a few inches from the most recent storm.

I had no trouble with my truck getting up the mountain, and I had chains for my tires when the weather gave off a real bite.

I slowed on the main road, the mountain pass.

Catching sight of a small car tinkering on the edge of the ravine, I put my truck in park and left the engine to idle and the lights on.

I reached for a flashlight and stepped out. I pulled my coat on and zipped it, as the night air was chilly.

If someone needed my help, I wanted to be prepared.

"Hello? Anyone in there?" I called out toward the vehicle. The windows were smashed, and the lights were off. There weren't any hazards flashing.

I shined my flashlight into the car. There was no sign of anyone inside. It was likely someone stopped by and picked up the driver.

Who in their right mind would drive that car up the mountain in winter?

It didn't have to be a snowstorm to know that you needed four-wheel drive and chains to make it through the snow. That didn't even consider when the rain washed out, the road or the ice storms made the road impassable.

I pointed my flashlight toward the ground.

There was a set of tracks, female footprints based on the heels and shoe size, and they headed for the main road. I shined the light farther down. The impressions continued, but my flashlight couldn't be seen after the turn in the road, a switchback.

Sighing, I headed to the truck, climbed back in, and was grateful for the warmth of shelter. Hopefully, whoever broke down was already picked up and on their way to town.

I put the truck in drive and shined my brights.

With my foot on the gas, I crept my vehicle up the mountain pass, my eyes on the main road and on the footprints buried in the snow, following them up the mountain. I didn't want to get distracted and miss if the person went off-trail.

Thankfully, she was smart enough to stay in the middle of the road.

I picked up speed a little, both antsy and worried. The last thing I wanted was someone to freeze to death because I took my time.

Another mile north and a figure lay in the road, dark, curled up, and not moving.

I left the car running.

It was a person, though I couldn't tell from the distance if she was alive. I assumed it was a woman based on the shoes.

I stepped closer.

She lay shivering on the snow-packed road. The woman was curled up, a gray-green knapsack and her purple coat blocking any evidence of an actual person as she attempted to bury herself to keep warm.

I cleared my throat, not wanting to startle the woman.

She didn't budge on my approach. That wasn't a good sign.

"Hello," I said and bent down, resting a hand on her back.

At least she was alive. Her body trembled against my hand. She was as cold as ice, and it was no wonder why.

I heard her try to speak, but I couldn't make out her words.

"I'm Jaxson," I said to her, trying to reassure the young woman that I didn't intend to cause her any harm. "Can you stand?"

Her words were mumbled and incomprehensible.

"I'm going to pick you up and carry you to my truck," I said.

She nodded slightly, and I breathed a sigh of relief that she was at least responsive, even if she was too cold to speak.

I scooped her up into my arms and carried her to my truck.

It only took a minute for me to open the passenger side door while holding her. I maneuvered her inside and hurried around to the driver's side door. I climbed into the truck and blasted even more heat on her. I cranked the temperature up to thaw the poor woman.

She shivered in the front of my truck. She'd been careless abandoning her car, walking at night in the cold, alone.

I reached into the backseat for an extra blanket I kept on hand for emergencies. This qualified as an emergency.

I unfolded the thick blanket and covered her body to help her get warm.

We were too far from the nearest hospital for her to be evaluated for frostbite. That was a solid two-hour drive in pleasant weather, and it meant passing the other side of the mountain where the weather was unpredictable.

"How long were you out there?" I asked.

I unzipped my coat and pulled it off my shoulders. The car was already warm and too hot for me.

She didn't seem to be overheated, so I left the thermostat alone and tried my best to make myself comfortable.

"A while," she said.

It was the first time I could understand the words coming past her lips. The tremble in her voice had vanished. She was quiet, and her hands shook as she held them in front of the heater.

I was afraid to suggest for her to remove her gloves, concerned about frostbite.

"I'm Jaxson Monroe," I said as I introduced myself to her again. She may not have heard me outside, or she did but didn't respond.

"Ariella Cole."

She smiled a bright and wide grin. Her cheeks were red, but at least they weren't bruised or discolored from the cold.

It could have been colder outside had it been the thick of winter. She was lucky.

"How are you feeling?" I asked.

I had a million questions, and the longer I stared at her, the more I realized how beautiful she was, in a very much girl-next-door kind of way.

Except there were no girls next door, and the number of women in Breckenridge was too few for my liking.

Honestly, I only needed one woman to care for, cherish, and take care of for the rest of my life. Of course, it wasn't that simple, nothing ever was.

Was it that I'd saved her made me want to protect her? No, I needed to protect her. I couldn't explain the all-encompassing feeling.

"A little warmer," she said as she glanced at me and gave me a faint smile. Her cheeks' red flame appeared to be from a soft blush instead of the cold this time.

I couldn't help but wonder why.

"Good. I'm glad I can get you a little warmer. If you can buckle yourself in, I'll get us back on the road and to town in no time."

I wasn't going anywhere without both of us being belted into the truck. Even with only a few inches of snow on the road, it was still dangerous. There were wild animals that could tear across the road at a moment's notice.

Ariella nodded, and her hands trembled, but she secured the seatbelt. I did the same and put the truck in drive.

We headed up toward Breckenridge.

I didn't ask her if that's where she was heading. If she stayed anywhere else, I'd find her a room for the night and deal with her situation tomorrow.

"To town," she said, her voice barely above a whisper.

"Yes, Breckenridge. Please tell me that's where you were heading." I hated to think she made a wrong turn and didn't have to travel up the dangerous mountain.

"It is. I just bought a place along the river. Though I imagine this time of year it's probably frozen."

"Any chance you bought it from Mason Reid?" I asked.

"Yes, how did you know?" Ariella asked.

"He's one of my former military buddies, my brother," I said. "I know exactly where you're staying. It's a nice place, small, and was gutted and renovated by yours truly. Well, Aiden and me."

"Who's Aiden?" Her eyes crinkled as she stared at me.

"Another one of my military buddies. Declan, Mason, Aiden, and I started a security firm, Eagle Tactical, a few years back."

I couldn't explain why I was so open to this woman, willing to divulge any secret if she asked. There was something about her. Was it the fact she was fresh meat, and I hadn't had a taste of her yet?

"All of you served together?" Ariella asked. She grinned and stared at me.

My heart fluttered in my chest, demanding to be set free. It had been a long time since anyone looked at me in that rare way.

I laughed, hoping for her not to notice the sexual tension brewing in the truck. As much as I wanted to act on it, I had some measure of self-control. We had just met. "We were all Special Forces with the Army."

With wide eyes, she grimaced as she removed her gloves. "Wow, a town of heroes."

I glanced at her long, thin fingers. They looked okay, albeit a little red, but there was no evidence of frostbite, which was good news.

"That is our motto," I said joking with her.

I returned my attention to the snow-covered road as we headed farther north and made the turn off for Breckenridge. "We don't have too much farther to go."

"Okay," she said. "That's good. Is there any place local to grab dinner? I'm starving, and I won't be able to go grocery shopping until my car gets pulled out of the ditch." Her voice was soft, wistful almost.

"I can take you over to Lumberjack Shack. They've got great food."

They were also the only place we could get in at nearly eight o'clock. It was late for the town, the bar was the only place open, and they didn't serve a decent dinner.

"Lumberjack Shack? I hope the food is better than the name."

"My buddy owns the place."

"Shit. I'm sorry," she said, quick to apologize. "That would be wonderful right now," she said.

She seemed to relax in the front seat and removed the blanket nestled around her body.

"Warm?" I asked.

That was a good sign after how cold and out of it she'd been earlier.

"Yes. Do you mind turning down the heat a bit?"

I adjusted the thermostat in the truck, hoping to make her a little more comfortable.

It was hot. Warm enough to make me want to strip down to my boxers and nothing else. I couldn't do that, not while driving and with a young lady in the truck.

"Thank you."

I pulled the truck down a gravel road and through the thick forest of trees before we slowed down to a crawl. "We're almost there," I said.

She reached for her bag and unzipped it to retrieve her purse.

I parked out front. The restaurant would ordinarily be closed on a Monday night, but I had a key. I helped Lincoln out from time to time, not with the cooking but tending the bar. Lincoln lived upstairs above the restaurant. He'd help me out, and well, if he didn't, I'm sure I could whip up something for her to eat.

"The place looks closed," she said.

The lights inside were dim, and there weren't any other vehicles parked around the front.

"It's after nine. Everything is closed at this hour. I have a key that can get us inside. Don't worry. It's not like there's an alarm system or anything to hack."

"Good, because I wasn't looking forward to spending my first night in Breckenridge in lockup," Ariella said.

"Come on." I climbed out from the truck and headed up the porch stairs and inside. I tried the door first, and it was locked. Pulling out my key for this very occasion and unlocking the door, I led her inside. "Ladies first."

She gave me a look, a cocked eyebrow, and a quirked grin. A beat later, she shrugged and stepped inside.

"It's beautiful," she said, having a look at the décor. "I'm sorry about what I said earlier. I get cranky when I'm hungry."

I bit my tongue to keep from commenting.

"I love the fact this place is a log cabin. It fits the bill of being a lumberjack shack."

It was apparent she was trying to make up for the insult she'd thrown out in the car. "I get a real Paul Bunyan vibe from this place. I'll bet the food is amazing too."

"It is some of the best in Montana. A real home-cooked meal from one of the top chefs in the area. If he didn't own the place, I'd worry someone else would steal him away," I said.

Truthfully, I'd been trying to steal him away to come work with the boys at Eagle Tactical full-time, but he wouldn't do it. He loved cooking too much to be back in the field permanently.

Heavy footsteps hit the stairs, and a moment later, Lincoln stepped into the restaurant.

"Jaxson, what are you doing here?" Lincoln asked.

While I may have been hungry, the look on Ariella's face told me she was starving.

"Grabbing some dinner. We haven't eaten yet, and I was hoping you'd make us something in the kitchen."

"The kitchen's closed, but for you and the pretty lady, I can make an exception," Lincoln said and grinned. "Where's Isabella? Shouldn't you be getting home to her? It's late."

Was he trying to kill any shot I had with Ariella? I didn't have a shot in hell, but I liked to think I did.

"At home, asleep." I didn't further elaborate. Why did my egg-headed military brother have to bring up Isabella?

"Do you have a menu?" Ariella asked Lincoln.

The way her eyes scoured over his body made my heart thump wildly in my chest.

I wanted her to look at me like that, not him.

Was I the jealous type? I never thought about it much, considering there weren't that many women to fawn over in town.

Lincoln smirked and rolled his eyes. "You're not one of those vegetarian types, are you?" He leaned in closer and whispered, "I can make one hell of a salad, but the bear around here is mighty tasty and to die for."

Her eyes widened in horror, and I tried not to laugh at Lincoln's joke. He usually wasn't quite so funny, but it seemed Ariella definitely wasn't from this side of the woods or even the state.

"I will have a salad," Ariella whispered. She sounded parched.

I couldn't help but stare at her, completely taken back by her beauty. Under the warm amber glow from the restaurant lighting, I finally got a good long look at her rosy complexion and freckles dusting her nose and cheeks. Her hair was dark and she had olive eyes that took my breath away.

She was gorgeous and not just because she was the newest resident of Breckenridge, and we didn't get a lot of ladies in town, let alone single ones.

However, I guessed that she was single. I had no idea.

I was just hoping she wasn't taken, given that she wasn't wearing a wedding band. That didn't mean anything, though. She could have been getting it sized.

Then again, if she was married, where was the bastard who let her drive to Breckenridge in that shitty car that couldn't make it up the mountain in winter? I'd kill him if he ever so much as hurt a hair on Ariella's head.

I exhaled a heavy sigh, not realizing how protective I'd become over a stranger. That's all she was, a young woman I'd rescued out in the cold. The thing was I wanted to know more about her. I wanted to discover who she was, why she was here, and well, if she was single and looking for a warm bed to crawl into.

I couldn't throw caution to the wind and sleep with her just because I had needs. No. Those days were over.

"Lincoln's just joking about eating bear. He makes a mean sandwich, and his stew is to die for."

"Stew. That sounds delicious," Ariella said. She rested her hands on the wooden table as we sat down. She removed her coat and hung it on the chair behind her.

"Okay, good. I'll fix you up something in the kitchen. Just sit tight and try not to fall victim to this one's lame attempts at flirting," Lincoln said, pointing at me.

I wanted to slug him.

"What brings you to Breckenridge?" I asked, watching her while my heart pitter-pattered in my chest.

While I knew she'd bought a cabin along the river, I didn't know why. Mason had said little other than he'd sold the place to an out-of-towner.

"Fresh start. I enjoy camping and thought what better place to live than the middle of nowhere."

I laughed, and while I doubted that was the entire story, if she didn't want to tell me, I wouldn't push the issue, either. "You picked the farthest corner of the world, didn't you?" I teased her. "Where are you from, Ariella?"

"New York, but I grew up in Nebraska," she said and held up a hand. "No Cornhusker jokes, please."

"I'm not sure I know of any." It was clear she wasn't a fan of Nebraska, not that I could blame her. I probably wouldn't like it much, either. I loved Breckenridge, though, and while winter could be brutal, it was also beautiful up here.

"Good," she said and laughed. Her eyes met the table before glancing back up at mine. "Can I ask you a question?"

I shrugged. "Go for it."

"Is Isabella your wife or girlfriend?"

She glanced down at my hand on the table.

I wasn't wearing a wedding ring, either, and it was obvious she was taking a long, hard look.

"No, she's my daughter."

CHAPTER THREE

ARIELLA

I'd wanted to ask him who Isabella was since the moment Lincoln brought up her name. I wasn't sure how to ask without completely prying or seeming nosey.

It had to be that he'd rescued me out in the cold, and I already had a sense of attachment to him. Wasn't there a name for that?

"You have a daughter?" That took me by surprise. It shouldn't have, as he was old enough to have kids. So was I.

"Yes, she's three years old." His expression seemed pained. His eyes crinkled just slightly before continuing to speak. "Her mom wanted to give her up for adoption and came to me, needing my signature to give up my rights as a father. I couldn't do it. I refused." His breathing deepened, and his ears reddened as he spoke.

I nodded as I listened to him tell me what happened.

"My options were full custody or give her up completely."

Lincoln brought two glasses of water to the table, giving Jaxson a look. "Dinner will be out soon," Lincoln said.

"Thank you," I said, glancing up at Lincoln before turning my attention back to Jaxson. "She's at home now, Isabella?"

"Yes. I have to depend on my brothers far more than I want to with raising Isabella, but they don't seem to mind." He laughed under his breath.

Had I missed the punchline? I didn't see what was so funny. "What's that?"

He smiled, shaking his head. "Forget it. It's not important."

I didn't quite understand what he wanted me to forget since I didn't know what he was talking about.

"Okay," I said, relieved that Lincoln was carrying our food over to the table. The delicious smell of stew wafted into the air as he brought two large bowls to the table, one for each of us. "Thank you."

"Anything else I can get for you?" Lincoln asked, staring directly at me.

Did he recognize me? The air had been sucked out of my lungs.

Jaxson opened his mouth. "We could use spoons."

"I'll get the lady a spoon. You can get yourself your silverware." He pointed at Jaxson. "Don't let this guy boss you around."

I feigned a smile. It had probably been my imagination. "Oh, I won't. Thanks for the tip," I said.

Lincoln headed toward the kitchen, grabbed two sets of silverware, and brought it over to the table.

"Thank you," Jaxson said before I could even voice the same sentiment.

"Let me know if you need anything else," Lincoln said before disappearing back into the kitchen.

"He knows how to make himself scarce," I said.

I reached for the spoon as the steam wafted from the bowl of soup. I took a sip, and my eyes closed. I relished the taste, the warmth, the fact it was a meal in my stomach.

I couldn't remember the last time I'd eaten today. The burnt coffee I picked up at the resort was stale and didn't count as a meal.

"Yeah. Lincoln's a good guy. Rough around the edges, and Isabella used to be terrified of him, but now they're best buds. Declan comes in a close second to Lincoln, which is funny because he spends more time with her. I swear he's ready to be a dad and settle down."

I took another bite of stew, grateful for the warm and comforting meal after a disastrous evening earlier. "Is Declan watching her now?"

Jaxson nodded between bites. "Yes. My brothers all take turns watching her when she's not at daycare. They're amazing. I couldn't do it without them." He sipped his water and glanced up at me. "So, you moved out here to get away, a change of scenery."

I nodded, not giving anything else away.

He couldn't know why I came to Breckenridge. I couldn't risk endangering him or his little girl.

"Any kids?" he asked.

"Not that I know of," I said, staring at him, trying hard not to laugh.

He grinned first and nodded. "Good one. You know what I do for a living. What about you?"

"Is this twenty questions?" I asked, trying to relax, but it wasn't the easiest task under his gaze. I couldn't tell him what I did for a living, or rather what I used to do.

Currently, I was unemployed. I knew he wasn't trying to be rude. This was probably how small-town people made small talk.

The thing of it was I might have been from New York, but my job took me all over the world. There were dangers in him knowing who I worked for and what I did. Hell, even Benjamin, my ex-husband, had no clue who he was married to.

I lived with secrets, slept with them, and recognized they were mine and mine alone.

"Sorry. Between my brothers and a toddler, I don't get a lot of opportunities to engage with a beautiful young woman."

The room grew warmer. Was I blushing? I glanced at the bowl of soup and pushed a strand of hair behind my ear. "I'll bet you're used to being a flirt. You are former military, and it shows."

He was no doubt gorgeous, with thick muscles behind his shirt. I'd worked with a few guys who had quite the physique, but the way he stared at me, it was clear I held his attention. It was flattering.

"Believe it or not, most of the town is married or one of my brothers."

"That can't be true." There were nearly nine hundred residents of Breckenridge, at least according to the internet.

I had researched the town thoroughly before moving here.

"You'll see," he said with a knowing grin.

I laughed under my breath.

I hoped there were more prospects in this town, not that Jaxson wasn't gorgeous on the eyes and had an incredible physique, but I also didn't want to throw myself at the first nice guy I met.

It had been a long time since I'd met any nice guys.

Ben, my ex-husband, was a bastard. The thought of marriage was like spoiled milk. I didn't want to go near it. I wasn't here looking to hook up or marry.

I never wanted to marry again. Once was enough. I wasn't even interested in dating, but with his gaze on me, my stomach in knots, I had to push those thoughts aside.

We finished our stew, and Lincoln came out of the kitchen to clean up the dishes. "How was it?" he asked me.

"Delicious! Do you always cook everything?" I asked. He may have owned the restaurant, but that didn't mean he ran the kitchen.

"Yes," Lincoln said, a glint in his eye. He appeared pleased by the compliment.

"I'll take the bill when you're ready," I said, not wanting to keep Jaxson out any later, especially knowing he had a daughter at home and a brother watching over her.

I intended to pick up his share of the meal too. After all, he'd saved my life earlier today. While I may not have been able to afford it, I'd figure it out.

"Your money's no good here."

"What?" I asked, confused.

Lincoln smiled. "It's on the house. Any friend of Jaxson eats free. At least for the first time. After that, we'll see what happens."

"Come on. Let me pay. This guy saved my life tonight. I can't leave knowing I owe both of you for your kindness."

Jaxson covered his mouth with his hand. He was grinning like an idiot, trying to hold back his laughter.

"What?" I asked, staring pointedly at Jaxson.

"You will not change his mind. Lincoln is the most stubborn of them all. Just say thank you and be done with it, or we'll never leave."

I glanced from Jaxson to Lincoln, staring up at him from where I sat at the table. He towered above. "Thank you," I said with genuine appreciation.

Lincoln gave a curt nod. "I'm sure I'll see you around. Jaxson, lock up the place on your way out. I'm going to clean up the kitchen and then head on upstairs."

"Will do, boss," Jaxson said, putting his hand back down on the table, grinning. "Are you ready to get out of here?"

I stood and grabbed my coat. No doubt I would need it back outside.

Pulling my jacket back on, I zipped up the teeth and then shoved my hands into my gloves.

I wasn't looking forward to the icy wind or the chill in the air outside, but it wouldn't be for long. We'd be in Jaxson's truck soon enough and then at the cabin.

Jaxson led me outside, his hand on the small of my back. I tried to hide the smile that shined right through me. Could he see it too? Was it that obvious that being around him made me at ease and free?

He walked me to his truck's passenger door and opened the door for me, offering me a hand inside. The truck was far taller than I was and reaching the running boards took a bit of a jump at my height. "Thank you."

"It's my pleasure," Jaxson said.

He waited for me to buckle before he shut the door and came around the truck to climb into the driver's side. He turned on the engine.

A welcoming blast of warm air hit my face. I pushed the vents away, grateful the truck hadn't cooled off since we stopped for dinner.

He pulled out of the lot and away from the restaurant. "Do you need to stop and pick up the key for the cabin?"

I'd already forgotten about the keys.

"Yes! The owner mentioned he left the keys in the mailbox but that it was at the end of the driveway. He made it sound rather far, like I'd need to drive down to get it."

"We'll grab it on the way up to the cabin," Jaxson said.

"Thank you. You think of everything, don't you?"

He smiled and laughed under his breath. His hands remained on the steering wheel, and his focus on the road.

He took his time as we headed farther north up the face of the mountain.

I gripped the side of the door as the switchbacks grew steeper and more challenging to see with each turn.

The headlights on the truck bounced back as a thin layer of fog hung in the air.

"Relax. I've got it. I take this route every day," he said, glancing at me.

"I know." I hadn't known, but I didn't want him to see through the fact that I was scared to death. Had it been obvious?

"Okay, stalker," he joked, smiling as he reached out, resting a hand on my arm. "I've driven through worse. Don't worry. You'll get the hang of it. Especially when you trade in your car for something a little more practical."

"Trade in my car? Do you think I totaled it?" I'd done a number on it, smashing the windows and denting the body when I had crashed into the tree.

He was right, and I needed to think about a more reliable vehicle for Breckenridge's roads, but how would I afford it?

Jaxson guided his hand back to the steering wheel. "Even if you got it fixed up, it still won't get you up the mountain in a blizzard."

"What about if my car had those metal things on the wheels?" I asked, trying to remember what they were called.

"Chains?"

"Yes, those." I hoped I could buy a set of chains and fix the car, and put off making payments on a new vehicle.

My income was tight. I'd spent every dime on that property and driving across the country to Montana. I didn't have a job lined up, and my wallet was near empty.

He lamented before answering. "I've never seen a car like yours around here."

I stared out the window, mesmerized by the beauty of the night.

We cleared the fog, which seemed strange since we'd traveled higher, but it appeared only to be a small patch along one section of the mountain.

In the distance, lights twinkled at the base of the mountain. A small town clustered together. "It's beautiful out here," I said as he slowed on the approach and turned off the road.

Jaxson rolled down his window as he came up to the mailbox and retrieved a set of house keys. "Here you go," he said, handing me the cold metal.

"Thank you." I took the keys with my gloved hands. As quick as he had opened the window, Jaxson shut it and put the truck in drive, heading down the narrow gravel road and through the forest.

I couldn't see anything except a few feet in front of us from the headlights. There was no sign of a cabin. "How much farther?" I asked.

"Another mile or two."

Snow crunched beneath the tires as we finally slowed on the approach. The lights were off, the cabin dark as night.

"I guess no one left the porch light on."

He laughed under his breath.

"What's so funny?" I asked, not seeing anything worth joking about.

From the outside, the wood exterior looked nice, well-kept, and rustic. It was indeed a log cabin, single-story and small, but the perfect size for one person. I didn't need anything big or pricy.

Besides, I couldn't afford anything else.

He shut off the engine of his truck and stepped outside in the cold air.

Jaxson didn't answer me. I climbed out from the truck, my shoes hitting the fresh snow piling up that hadn't been shoveled.

His vehicle had driven through it with ease, but I trampled through the slush and up the porch steps covered in ice.

"Be careful," Jaxson warned, his breath on my neck as he followed me up the steps, a hand on my lower back.

Was he trying to make sure I didn't fall, or was the proximity something else far more intimate?

Already, I enjoyed being around him, but that was dangerous. I barely knew the guy, and he had a kid.

Talk about complicated.

That didn't even include the fact that there was a bounty on my head.

There were several people who wanted me dead. Living in the middle of nowhere was supposed to protect me, but would it?

"Do you have the key?"

"Yes," I said, trying the front door key that Jaxson had retrieved earlier from the mailbox. It slid into the lock easily and turned.

I pushed open the door, expecting it to be warm and inviting. It certainly wasn't warm.

I shivered and reached for the wall, looking for a light switch. Nothing. "It's freezing."

"The cabin uses a wood-burning stove to heat the place." He stalked right for the stove and bent down. He grabbed a few logs kept dry out of the snow and worked on the fire. Jaxson stacked the wood and struck a match, and it slowly caught ablaze.

"You know your stuff," I said, watching him with curiosity.

It had been years since I'd lit a fire like that. The last house had a gas fireplace that involved flipping a switch. I wasn't so lucky out here. However, the wood-burning stove would be a lot warmer. "What about the lights?"

He headed toward the bed, just a few feet away from the fire that roared to life.

The open floor plan offered no real privacy, but I hoped it would help heat the space evenly.

The cabin had come fully furnished, which was nice since I had little with me. Most of it had been sold in New York. Everything else of mine was stuffed into the trunk of my car.

"Here you go." Jaxson grabbed a flashlight style lantern and handed it to me. "Keep a few extra sets of batteries on hand."

The smile fell from my face. "You're joking." He had to be kidding with me.

The cabin had electricity, right?

I had wanted to live off grid, but I hadn't actually intended to live primitively.

"About what?"

"There's seriously no electric in this place?" I couldn't believe it! How could his buddy sell me a house that didn't have electricity? It hadn't been mentioned—one way or the other—on the listing online.

"You bought a cabin in the woods. You're lucky it has indoor plumbing."

CHAPTER FOUR

JAXSON

I may not have known Ariella that well, but it didn't take a mind reader to see she was pissed.

Her hands were balled up at her sides, her jaw tight and brow furrowed. She breathed heavily and loudly, although that could have been from the fact it was cold in the cabin, and she was chilled.

While I needed to get home to Isabella, I also didn't want to leave Ariella alone, in the cold and dark. If I'd have known earlier in the day that she was arriving, I'd have stopped by and started the fire in the stove.

The cabin was frigid, and it would take hours to warm it up to a decent temperature.

"I can't believe this," she said, pacing the length of the room, her feet heavy on the wooden floorboards. "I would never have moved here if I knew there wasn't electricity. How am I supposed to survive without a refrigerator?"

I wanted to tell her to relax. Was that the wrong answer? I hated when the guys told me to chill out.

"I'll bring my generator over, and we can hook it up to a refrigerator. We'll have to go into town in the morning and pick one out. I can drive it back and sent it up for you."

She groaned.

"You didn't notice the lack of a fridge in the pictures?"

Her lips pursed, and her eyes narrowed. "I may have been in a rush to buy considering the price. Now I see why it was affordable."

She rubbed at her forehead and slowly removed her gloves.

"Listen, why don't you come back with me tonight? Stay over at my place for a few hours until your cabin gets toasty. Then I can drive you back, or you can walk home. It's not far between our properties. There's a bridge that goes over the river. I live just on the other side of it."

She exhaled a heavy breath, and her tongue darted out, licking her lips. "We're neighbors."

"That's right," I said. "What do you say? I can bring by the generator in the morning, and we can go into town and pick up a new fridge."

She stalled and shifted her weight on her feet.

Was there another option that I wasn't considering? I didn't know of anyone giving away a free refrigerator, and the nearest thrift shop was hours away and never carried appliances. It was unlikely anyone had a spare refrigerator, though freezers were easier to come by since many of the townies were hunters and stored meat in the freezers.

"I'll be fine tonight. It's been a long day. I should probably just crawl up under the blankets and head to bed."

"If you're sure." I didn't want to push her. "There are extra blankets in the closet if you're cold. Do you have a phone? I can give you my number in case you need anything."

She slowly unzipped her coat. "It's dead. I need to charge it, but that seems an impossible task." Ariella yawned and brought her hand up to her lips as if she could hide the gesture.

"I'll bring you a solar charger in the morning. I have a spare." I stepped back toward the door, not wanting to overstay my welcome.

It was late. My daughter was at home and needed me.

"Thank you."

I headed for the door. "If you need anything, I'm just over the bridge. It's not too far a walk."

"I'll be fine, but I appreciate it."

"Lock up after I leave. Most people don't lock their doors in Breckenridge, but you shouldn't make that a habit." I'd seen too much in my day to leave a door unlocked.

She quirked an eyebrow. "Is there something I should know?"

Her eyes were bright and wide, a deep olive that matched her sweater. I wanted to step closer, lean in to touch her shoulder, and reassure her she would be fine, but we barely knew one another, and I wasn't one to make empty promises.

"It's just better to be safe than sorry," I said.

It wasn't anything specific or anyone who caused trouble.

In the middle of nowhere, being in the woods led to a few individuals with dark pasts hiding out and keeping off-grid. While they never bothered me, I couldn't say the same for a pretty young girl, all alone.

I'd have to keep an eye on her and make sure she was safe.

"I'll see you tomorrow." I headed outside and waited until I heard the click of the lock before hurrying down the porch stairs and to my truck.

Fresh snow fell, and I climbed into my truck and headed back the way I came, on the same narrow road that led to her house. I would have to travel back to the main road, then head another mile or so north before the next turnoff. While our houses were close, the distance and drive to get there was a lot longer than by foot.

The higher north I traveled, the more snow seemed to fall. It was blustery cold the moment I stepped out of the truck.

I hurried inside my house, a two-story log cabin, and removed my coat and shoes. The hearth was lit, offering warmth and an ambient glow to the living room where Declan lay asleep.

He snored softly. A checkered flannel blanket covered him. He had stretched out on the sofa, taking up the entire length.

I didn't have the heart to wake him.

Declan was a good friend, helping me out with Isabella. While he didn't have any kids of his own, it was obvious he wanted them and would make a great father one day.

With the lights already off, I locked up the house and quietly headed up the stairs to check on Izzie.

Curled up in her bed, she stirred as I entered the room.

I held my breath, not wanting to awaken my baby girl. I watched over her for a long moment before finally tiptoeing out of her room and into mine.

Exhausted, I collapsed onto the mattress, not bothering to undress further.

At least my shoes were downstairs by the front door. There was no way I could do much else.

I shut my eyes, prepared to let sleep win when a loud crash vibrated through the house. It came from downstairs.

"Declan?"

On high alert, I hurried out of bed and grabbed my gun from the safe.

I'd do whatever was necessary to protect my little girl.

Quietly, I headed down the stairs, one step at a time, to make sure the intruder couldn't hear me.

Gun drawn, I kept my back to the wall of the stairwell.

Coming around the corner, Declan gasped and held up his hands in surrender. "Careful, Jax. Don't shoot."

"What the hell was that?" I asked, lowering the barrel of the gun as I turned on the safety.

"Avalanche. Earthquake. Who the hell knows?" Declan said. He rubbed at his eyes and ran a hand through his short-cropped, dark hair. "Woke my ass up, and clearly, it did yours as well."

I doubted it was an avalanche or earthquake based on the sound. "I wasn't asleep."

"You came home late," Declan said.

"Did you get my text from the restaurant?"

"Yes. Lincoln called and told me all about the pretty girl you were having dinner with. So, who is she?"

Declan headed for the fridge and grabbed himself a beer, bringing it to the sofa to have a seat. He was awake and expecting to converse.

I wasn't in the mood for a drink.

I put the gun on the coffee table and sat down on the sofa with my brother. "Ariella. She's the new buyer of the cabin on the river, my next-door neighbor."

Declan smiled, and his grin widened. "Is she as hot as Lincoln made her out to be?"

I tried my best not to grin, but it was hard not to reveal at first glance how she made me feel. Being around her made my heart soar like a balloon high above the clouds.

"You're smitten," Declan said and laughed under his breath.

I didn't need my friends ganging up on me and teasing me about Ariella. It was likely that I'd see her again, and not just tomorrow morning.

"I was just being friendly and helping a neighbor out," I said, trying my best to change the subject. "By the way, she had no idea the cabin didn't have electric."

"Damn," Declan said. He sipped his beer. "I'll bet she was pissed when she found out."

That was an understatement.

"Yeah. I offered her my generator, and I was going to go into town with her in the morning and bring back a fridge. She's going to need to do something if she plans on living here year round."

"You don't have to take care of her, Jax. She's a grown woman," Declan said.

I knew that, but I didn't care. In part, it was my responsibility. I always seemed to clean up after my buddies made a mess of things.

I was the responsible one.

"I realize that," I said and stood.

I didn't need a lecture from Declan. He was younger than me, only by a year, but it still irked me when he tried to give me advice.

"Who'd you think was going to buy the place?" Declan asked.

"Honestly, I thought it'd be some rich folks from California. Some lavish city people who wanted a second home in seclusion, off-grid, where they could spend a few weeks a year in the outdoors."

"That was wishful thinking. No one comes out here for just the summer. Well, almost no one."

I sighed and stood.

The unspoken name he was referring to was the mother of my baby girl.

Emma was a summer fling, a woman who had come to Breckenridge to get away from her wild city life and unwind for the summer.

She'd done more than relax. She'd found her way into my bed and ended up pregnant.

"Sorry, I didn't mean to bring her up," Declan said.

He knew I hated talking about her. It wasn't that I was in love with the woman; it had no doubt been a summer fling for both of us, but I hadn't been too fond of hearing she planned on giving up Isabella for adoption. Showing up on my doorstep, it hadn't been to tell me she was pregnant or ask about my involvement.

No.

She'd shown up that day to ask me to sign my parental rights away, something I refused to do.

"I'm going to head out, get a few hours of sleep before work," Declan said. "Do you need me for anything else before I go?"

"Tomorrow, on your way down the mountain pass, Ariella's car ended up in a ditch. Can you pull it out and tow it over to the shop? I'm not sure it's in mountain weather shape, but she's going to need something to get her around town. Also, find her a pair of used chains she can put on her tires to get her up the mountain. Let me know what they cost and I'll cover it."

"You got it." Declan owned the tow shop in town.

When we decided to start Eagle Tactical, he hired out help, bringing in a mechanic and a crew to support him.

"You're welcome to stay and crash on the couch. It's snowing out there, but I know that's never stopped you before."

It was late, and while the snow had just started coming down within the past hour, it likely hadn't lightened up any.

Declan grabbed his beanie and jacket, pulling the thick material over his shoulders before zipping his coat. He slipped on a pair of boots and then donned his gloves.

"Have fun tomorrow with the new girl." He winked at me.

"Her name is Ariella," I said, correcting him.

"Whatever. I hear from Lincoln she's cute, and the blush on your ears gives it away that you like her. I can't wait to meet her. If you don't sink your teeth into her, I might have to."

"It's time for you to go." I ushered him out the door and shut it behind him. I ran a hand through my hair, gasping for breath.

Just the thought of Declan trying to steal her away pained me.

Why was that?

She wasn't mine. She wasn't anyone's, well, as far as I knew. She hadn't exactly told me her story, why she was in Breckenridge, and whether or not she was single—not that I was looking.

I was a father, which came first and foremost.

I took the gun back upstairs and secured it in the safe before stripping down to my boxers for bed.

I climbed under the covers; morning would come soon enough, and my little girl would wake me at the crack of dawn.

For a few scant hours, I could dream of Ariella, of her smile and laugh, and let the nightmares that haunt me vanish in the night.

CHAPTER FIVE

ARIELLA

I had trouble sleeping. At first, it had been the cold air and being in an unfamiliar place. While it might have been my home, it wasn't warm and cozy.

My fingers and toes were chilled beneath the thick blankets, and I'd dug out every extra comforter and quilt that I could find in the linen closet.

Halfway through the night, I threw the rest of the wood into the fire, stoking it to keep the cabin warm.

Sometime later, I no longer needed the blankets and had fallen asleep to the blazing hearth.

I stirred awake, hearing the crunch of tires outside and an engine idle. What time was it?

"Ariella." He knocked briskly.

"Just a second," I said from the bed. The covers were tangled, and half of the blankets were on the floor. The room was stuffy.

I pushed myself out of bed and didn't flinch like I'd expected as my bare feet touched the wood floor. The cabin was warmer than the previous night.

I unlocked the door and pulled it open. A blast of cold air smacked me in the face and forced me to take a step back.

"Holy hell, it's hot in here," Jaxson said.

He hurried toward the wood-burning stove and pointed at the bare spot where firewood had been stacked the previous night.

"Did you burn the entire lot?"

"Was I not supposed to?" We were in the forest and there had to be more lying around.

"It has got to be a hundred degrees in here."

Sweat licked his forehead, and he removed his hat and gloves. His eyes moved over my body, reminding me I had slept in my clothes from the previous night.

I didn't have any extra clothes in my knapsack. My belongings were in the car's trunk, abandoned halfway down the mountain.

He had to be exaggerating. "It's not that hot."

He stepped farther inside the cabin, pointing at a thermometer gauge affixed to the wall. "Look at this," Jaxson said.

I didn't want to look at it and see that he was right. "It's hard to tell, given there's no electricity."

Jaxson snorted under his breath and stalked toward the front window and yanked open the curtains. "Now you can see, and you don't need a flashlight."

He was getting under my skin. It hadn't been his fault about the cabin, but it didn't help my mood.

I slipped on my heels, not the most sensible in this weather, but my boots were back in the vehicle. Grumbling under my breath, I grabbed my coat from the hook near the door.

"I want you to take me to your buddy, the one who sold me the cabin." I grabbed my keys and purse and yanked the door open and turned back. "What are you waiting for?" I asked.

He let out a heavy sigh before following me out the door.

I stomped through the snow, partially because I was wearing heels and also because I was pissed. My feet were freezing.

I pulled my jacket closed so that he wouldn't see my discomfort.

Suckered into thinking I'd gotten a great deal on a home when, in reality, I'd been played like a fool. I was going to give it to his friend, the lashing that he deserved!

I waited outside his truck. The engine was on, but the doors were locked.

Another minute, and he was at the truck, unlocking the doors and letting me inside. "Thanks," I said, climbing inside the warmth of the cabin.

"Hi," a small voice squeaked from the backseat. My eyes widened and I spun around to see who was in the truck.

"See, Daddy didn't take too long," Jaxson said to the toddler in the backseat. "Ariella, I'd like you to meet my daughter, Isabella."

"Hi, Isabella," I said, giving her a forced smile. She was cute, with her daddy's eyes and deep mahogany hair.

I didn't want to smile. I wasn't happy. Anger bubbled through me as I attempted to buckle my seatbelt. My hands trembled.

Isabella's smile beamed, oblivious to the tension in the truck between us.

"Are you taking me to Mason's house?" I asked.

"He's at work right now," Jaxson said. He rested his hands on the steering wheel but didn't put the truck into reverse.

We sat in the driveway, in front of the cabin, awkwardly.

I knew why I was pissed. It had everything to do with his friend. But why did Jaxson seem unsettled? "So, take me to his work."

That was the easiest solution. I'd give him a piece of my mind, and perhaps I could get the house stuff sorted.

Though I wasn't sure how it would get fixed. Even if he gave me back the money and took possession of the property, I had nowhere else to live. A hotel would be costly, and another property at that price was unheard of.

I should have known the price was too good to be true, but I was eager to move and optimistic.

I was a sucker.

Isabella made clicking sounds with her tongue in the truck's backseat. Her feet swung, and every so often, the tips of her toes would hit my seat.

Jaxson spun around, his hand falling onto her leg. "No kicking the seat, Izzie." He was gentle but firm with his daughter. The way he paid her attention warmed my heart.

Inwardly, I groaned. I didn't want to notice him in that way.

Yes, he was gorgeous and probably had an impressive body under his jacket and jeans, but I was newly divorced. I wasn't looking for love or even a fling.

Besides, he had a daughter which no doubt complicated matters further, not to mention my past.

He huffed under his breath before he finally put the truck into reverse. "Fine. If you want me to take you to Mason, I'll drive you there."

"That's all I'm asking," I said. I sat quietly, staring out the side window and paying attention to the route. I did not know where anything was located, and as Jaxson drove us down from the direction we came, he turned off the road a few miles down.

If I remembered correctly, we traveled in the restaurant's opposite direction, but it was nearby.

Jaxson pulled up outside a large brick complex.

Smoke billowed in waves from the chimney. He put the truck in park and glanced back at his daughter.

"Daddy will be right back." He left the engine running and locked the doors, shoving his keys into his pocket.

I was envious of his keyless entry and remote start. My vehicle was crap compared to the massive truck that he drove.

"Okay. Let's go," I said as I stalked up the stairs of the small building. A sign just outside the door read Eagle Tactical.

So, this was where Jaxson worked.

I opened the door and stepped inside the building. A young woman sat at a desk near the front of the entryway.

"Can I help you?" she asked, her tone bubbly and wearing a plastered smile. She looked every bit fake.

"I'm here to speak with Mason," I said. I didn't elaborate on the reason for my visit.

She frowned, flipping open her scheduling calendar. She glanced over the individual slots and pages. I hadn't given her my name. Was she looking for a name she didn't recognize on the calendar?

Jaxson came up from behind. She mustn't have seen him when he first entered the building.

"Good morning, Lucy."

"Mr. Monroe, I didn't see you come in," Lucy said. "How is little Isabella doing?"

"She's good. Thank you. Is Mason in his office? Ariella would like a word with him."

Lucy stood and sauntered off down the hallway. She knocked before opening a door and poking her head in, presumably giving him the message.

I shifted on my feet, the snow dripping down and making a mess on the wood floor. I didn't wipe my feet very well when I came inside.

She cleared her throat and gestured us to follow her down the hall.

I went first, my feet clicking hard against the wooden floor with each step. Jaxson was just a few feet behind me on my heel.

The hallway was freshly painted toasted oatmeal, but the boards beneath were wood. The building looked updated recently.

"Can I help you?" Mason asked. He sat behind his desk, buried behind a mess of paperwork, his attention on his computer and not the least bit on me.

"I'm Ariella Cole. You sold me the cabin just up the road." I assumed he knew the address and that he wasn't making it a habit of buying and selling shady properties.

"That's right, a real gem." His brow furrowed, and he glanced past me. "Good morning, Jaxson." He pushed the chair back from the desk and stood.

"The property you sold me was misrepresented. It doesn't have electricity, and you failed to make that apparent before signing the papers."

I stepped farther into the small, overcrowded office. An ugly green, dented file cabinet sat nestled beneath the window. Above it was another stack of manila folders waiting to be filed.

"Jaxson, do you want to give me a hand?" Mason asked, gesturing at me.

"Excuse me?" I asked.

I didn't need to be handled.

"I'm not the problem," I said, my hands in fists at my side. I needed to control the anger raging inside of me before I did something I'd regret. "Your listing neglected to point out that there was no electricity and no heat on the property."

Mason took a step closer toward me. "Now hold on right there, Missy. The cabin has heat. If you don't know how to chop firewood or bring in logs and need a man to do it for you, that's not my problem."

I pulled back my fist to land a blow to Mason's cheek, but Jaxson grabbed my arm and guided it back down to my side forcefully. "Get off me," I said, shrugging out of his grasp. I didn't need to be man-handled.

"You need to take your girlfriend and go," Mason said. He pointed at the door.

How dare he!

"I'm not his girlfriend." I didn't need to explain to Mason how we met.

Besides, they were colleagues and military brothers. He'd probably find out soon enough.

Weren't small towns full of gossip?

"You owe me for misrepresenting the cabin." I stood my ground, my feet planted in front of him. I wasn't leaving.

"I don't owe you a damned thing, lady," Mason said. "The listing called the place 'quiet, rustic living'. There's no lie in that phrase, and the fact you neglected to see if it had electricity is not my fault. Many cabins in the woods out here are used as a second property for a weekend getaway. Besides, if anyone is to blame, Jaxson dealt with the listing. I only approved it."

"Excuse me?" That caught me off guard. What did he mean, Jaxson dealt with the listing?

Was he a realtor too? Didn't he work here, at Eagle Tactical?

"You always did like to throw me to the wolves," Jaxson said. He folded his arms across his chest, his eyes narrow as he glared at Mason.

I scoffed and spun around on my heel, mouth agape as I stared up at Jaxson. "Are you calling me a wolf?"

"If the shoe fits, honey," Mason said from behind me.

I wanted to kill that smug bastard. I ignored Mason for a second and tried to regain my composure.

Jaxson towered above me. His eyes locked on mine, and I realized he never answered the question. He was avoiding it.

Hell, I probably would be too if I were standing in his shoes. "Are you responsible for the listing?"

He cleared his throat, but he didn't answer me, only stared into my eyes. I swallowed the lump that formed in my throat.

"We should get back out to the car. I left Izzie in there, and it's been long enough," Jaxson said and hurried down the hall like a hurricane, leaving me standing there with Mason.

Was he trying to get away from me or avoid answering the question? Perhaps he was inclined to do both. I groaned and heard Mason chuckling behind me. "You'd better go catch him before he leaves you in the cold and dust. I know I would."

"God, you're an ass," I muttered on my way out of his office and rushed to the car.

Jaxson sat in the truck's cabin waiting for me. I climbed into the passenger side and buckled up. I shot him a look that said, 'fuck you.'

I was no longer in the mood to talk. It didn't help that his adorable little girl was seated behind us, singing Disney princess songs.

"You're mad. Let me explain," Jaxson said.

"Can you? Do you mean it wasn't intentional?" I found it difficult to believe that he just forgot to include that little tidbit in the listing.

While he seemed like a nice guy, he was a jerk just like Mason.

He answered me calmly as he turned to face me, the truck still in park. "I offered to help Mason list the cabin. That was my mistake, and the few dollars he gave me for helping, I swear it's all yours."

Was he trying to make me feel bad? I was short on cash, like really short, where my bank account was drained and all I had was a couple of ones left in my wallet.

I still needed to fix my car and now install electricity in the cabin. That had to cost a fortune! I wasn't rich, and this wasn't my second home.

"I don't want your money." I could use it, but I wasn't about to tell him that minor fact.

He had a daughter, and kids were expensive. I would not take his money.

That jerk Mason, I would have gladly snatched from his greedy little palms, but that didn't seem a likely scenario.

Jaxson stared at me, his gaze unwavering. "Okay. How about I take you into town and buy you a fridge and generator?"

"Are you serious? I don't need handouts." It was precisely what I needed to survive and live in that rustic cabin, but I didn't want to seem desperate.

CHAPTER SIX

JAXSON

She hated me, not that I blamed her. I'd been completely incompetent in listing the cabin.

Ariella was right.

I had neglected to put that it didn't have electricity but only because it never crossed my mind. I needed to make it up to her, and the most logical way was to help her with the fridge and generator.

While I intended to loan her one for the short term, the truth was she needed one until the place was hooked up to the grid.

"I promise what I'm offering isn't a handout. It's just me doing something neighborly," I said, trying to reason with her. "We are neighbors, Ariella. I'm going to be seeing a lot more of you whether you like it or not."

She groaned and ran a hand through her long brunette hair.

I kept my attention on the road as I drove us down the mountain and into town. It would be an all-day event, and I didn't even bother asking if she had other plans. I assumed she didn't, other than getting her car towed out of the ravine and fixed up.

Ariella stared out the window, her voice soft and barely audible over Isabella's loud singing. "Thank you," she whispered.

"Of course," I said. I wanted to keep her talking, to learn about her, what she was doing in Breckenridge. "I hope I'm not keeping you from other plans you might have had for today."

"Just some unpacking and retrieving my car. I need to call a tow truck, but my phone is still dead," she said. "There isn't a phone in the house, so I'm going to need another favor."

"Another favor?" I joked with her. "You're going to owe me pretty soon."

She groaned under her breath.

"It's not that bad," I said. "Besides, I talked to Declan last night when I got home. He should have it in the shop later this afternoon."

"Thank you."

She'd never been here before and was probably trying to escape something or someone.

Most people who ventured to the middle of nowhere did so because they had secrets to hide.

I was overthinking it.

I'd been in the military in my younger years and had seen a lot that left a lasting impression.

In my day-to-day work for Eagle Tactical, I dealt with all of it, everything from kidnappings and ransom drops to human trafficking. We work closely with the local police department and county sheriff.

"You never told me what you do for a living." I wasn't trying to pry, but I was curious all the same. It came with the job, digging into people's lives.

"Yeah, I guess you could say I'm unemployed at the moment. I had an interview yesterday afternoon at Blue Sky Resort, but I'm not sure when I'll hear anything back. Any chance Lincoln is looking to hire a waitress?"

Lincoln kept the overhead on his restaurant as low as possible, which meant he wasn't usually open to new hires. "I can ask him, but you'd have better luck at Blue Sky, especially this time of year."

"Any chance you know the owner?" she asked. "Maybe you could put in a good word for me?"

"Daddy, I'm hungry," Isabella whined from the backseat.

I glanced back at Isabella over my shoulder and then at Ariella. "Can you open the glove box?"

"Yeah, sure." She leaned forward and unclasped the glove box, revealing a bag of pretzels. "How old are these?" Ariella laughed and pulled the baggie out.

"A week or two, max. It's fine." I snatched the baggie from Ariella, opened it, and handed it back to Isabella. "Here you go. We'll get lunch in a bit, Izzie."

She munched loudly as she ate her pretzels in the backseat. Her feet were kicking but just missing the seat.

I glanced back at her. No doubt she was bored with being in the truck and needed time to run around.

"We'll be there soon," I said, trying to assure her it wouldn't be too much longer in the truck.

Ariella glanced out the side window, quiet and lost in her thoughts.

"I'm sorry. You were saying?" I hated how quickly I could get distracted.

Ariella shifted in her seat, staring at me, her undivided attention entirely focused on me. "I was just wondering if you knew the owners of Blue Sky Resort. I *really* need a job."

The emphasis on *really* made my stomach clench.

How bad off was she?

I hadn't seen her belongings, and I assumed everything she owned was in her car since she bought the cabin fully furnished.

Another reason I had believed the owner was looking for a second house, a temporary getaway for a vacation.

"I don't, but if they don't hire you, let me know, and I will ask around."

She wouldn't be without a job for long. The community of Breckenridge was small but tight-knit and helped one another out.

"Thank you."

"Daddy, I'm bored," Isabella said. She tossed the empty bag on the floor of the truck, the crumbs spilling out with it.

"I know, baby girl." I pulled up to the front of the big box hardware store and parked the truck before I helped Izzie out of her car seat and carried her on my hip. Together, the three of us headed inside and out of the cold.

"They sell refrigerators here?" Ariella asked, following beside me. I could tell she was hurrying to keep up.

"All major appliances," I said, leading her down an aisle and toward the back of the store. "It shouldn't take too long, and then we can grab lunch and head back home."

"You know your way around this place."

"We do enough shopping here to keep this location open," I joked, walking her toward the appliance section. It wasn't difficult to find the refrigerators, and we walked up and down the aisle twice. "See anything you like?"

She shuffled her feet, and every time we walked past one nicer than the next, her eyes widened as she balked at the sticker. "I could buy a new car at this price!"

I tried not to laugh.

I understood her predicament. She was out of work and concerned about the financial aspect of buying a new household appliance. There was no way she could buy a decent vehicle that would get her up the mountain and safely around town for the cost of a refrigerator.

I held my tongue, trying to think of another store, a different place that might be more affordable, with fewer bells and whistles, so to speak.

She paced the aisle once, twice, and by the third time, she stopped in front of a mini fridge.

"I can probably afford this one," she said. "If I put it on my credit card." She seemed to talk to herself, or she was talking to me, but her voice had dropped so much that I'd barely heard her remark, but I had heard it.

I came up beside her, Izzie growing restless on my hip. Reluctant to put her down, I didn't want her running off and tearing through the store, getting into trouble. She was fast and spritely.

"Listen," I said to Ariella. "I offered to cover the cost of your refrigerator, and I meant it."

"You shouldn't have to do that," she said, folding her arms across her chest. "It's not your fault I fucked up."

"Fucked. Fucked. Fucked," Izzie repeated what Ariella said.

Ariella's olive eyes widened in horror. "Oh, my gosh! I'm so sorry," she said, quick to apologize.

It was clear she wasn't used to being around kids.

"You shouldn't say that, Isabella." Ariella looked horrified, and for a good reason, but I let out a loud sigh.

"She's heard worse from the guys." However, I gave them hell when they cursed in front of my little girl.

I didn't have it in me to do the same to her.

"That's no excuse," she said. "Again, I'm so sorry."

"Apology accepted."

I didn't want her stressing over what she'd done. Mistakes happened. We'd all made them, and Izzie was bound to hear far worse things in her lifetime.

"Back to the refrigerator," I said, nodding toward the appliances. "Do you want to pick one out, or should I do it for you?"

She chewed her bottom lip, her eyes filled with trepidation. What was she worried about?

I had offered to pay and was intending on making good on my promise. Mason may have sold her the cabin, but I should have been more careful in its listing. She should have realized there wasn't a fridge, but I had neglected to include details about electricity. Had the roles been reversed, I'd have flipped out too.

"Sure, if you want to buy me a fridge, you can buy me this one," she said, pointing at the mini fridge that couldn't even hold a case of water. It was cheap, certainly within my budget too, but it wouldn't do her any good at home to store her groceries.

I headed down the aisle, glancing at the appliances once more before stopping at the end cap and examining a floor model.

Its bright yellow sticker was an affordable price and offered a 60-day warranty. Hopefully, that would be sufficient.

"What about this one?" It was still more than her mini fridge, but she more than likely could afford it if she wouldn't let me pay. Though I fully intended on purchasing the fridge for her.

"That'll do." We found a cashier and had them ring up the item.

I pulled out my credit card, handing it to the cashier before Ariella could offer her own form of payment.

"Thank you," she said to me as we loaded it into the bed of the truck, tied it down, and then headed into town for lunch.

Izzie behaved incredibly well for the afternoon. I knew how bored she was, but she seemed quite mesmerized by Ariella.

Izzie sat beside me in the booth. While we waited for our food to come, she climbed under the table and snuck over to sit next to Ariella.

"Hey there," Ariella said, smiling at Isabella. "Do you want to keep me company?"

Izzie shook her head, her eyes bright and wide.

She climbed onto the seat, sitting on her knees, so she had a little extra height. Her hands reached out, playing with Ariella's hair, touching her.

"Izzie," I said, warning her to behave. Not everyone liked to be touched by a toddler.

"She's okay," Ariella said with a grin, glancing at me. She didn't seem to mind, or if she did, she pretended it didn't bother her. "How old are you?" she asked Izzie, although I'd already told her yesterday.

"Three," she said, holding out three fingers proudly to announce her age. "How old are you?"

"Izzie." I laughed, trying to scold her, but it was difficult when she had that adorable look in her eyes, that twinkle of both mischievous and delight that made her even more loveable. "We don't ask grownups their age."

"Okay," Izzie said and rolled her eyes.

"Oh, my gosh. She's already a teenager," I said.

I couldn't believe the eye roll. She had to have learned it from someone, but I wasn't sure where she'd picked it up. She'd spent quite a bit of time with Declan, and he had a few nasty habits, but I hadn't witnessed that one previously.

Izzie scrunched her nose while smiling. "Do you have a boyfriend?" she asked Ariella.

"I do not have a boyfriend," she said, matter of factly, before I could even tell Izzie to cool it. "What about you?" Ariella asked, teasing Isabella. "Do you have a boyfriend?"

Izzie violently shook her head. "Gross! Boys are icky!"

I laughed under my breath. At least that answer settled my nerves. "Good, keep saying that."

I didn't want her thinking about boys and boyfriends, or girlfriends. She was much too young to be thinking about crushes and what came along with that.

"What about you?" Ariella asked, scrunching her nose up and smiling just like Izzie had done a moment earlier. "Do you have a girlfriend?" she asked me.

While I knew she was playing games and entertaining my daughter, which I was grateful for, was she also asking because she was interested, or was I reading into it? I wanted her to be asking because she liked me, not because she was just putting me on the spot. Though, why did I care how she felt? We barely knew one another.

"Do you want to be his girlfriend?" Izzie asked.

"I don't think it quite works like that," I said, glaring at Izzie. She didn't seem to take the hint. Her mouth opened about to say something else that would inevitably embarrass me further.

"Sure, it does," Ariella said. She was wearing a 100-watt smile, her eyes shining as she didn't seem to take her gaze off of me.

Lincoln brought out three plates from the kitchen, interrupting the moment. I wasn't sure whether to kiss him or kill him.

Izzie snuck back under the table and climbed onto the seat beside me to eat. I cut up her lunch into small, bite-sized pieces and watched as she grabbed each bite with her hands, foregoing a fork. We'd have to work on that at some point.

"Saved by the bell," Ariella said, the smile more subdued, but she seemed at ease, happier, carefree. Her shoulders relaxed, and the tension seemed to slip out of her body as she ate her salad.

I helped Izzie with her meal before digging in on my burger. I hadn't realized how hungry I'd been or how late the afternoon had gotten.

It was any wonder Izzie hadn't melted down.

When the bill came, I wouldn't let Ariella pay, although she offered. Knowing she didn't have a job, whatever money she had, she probably needed far more than I did right now. "You'll pay after you get hired at the lodge," I said. I hoped the job came through for her.

"Fine, but then you're buying the drinks. You said there's a bar around town, right?"

It had been ages since I'd gone out on a date. However, she hadn't exactly called us going out a date. I was reading too much into her intentions. We were friends, neighbors, and I was supposed to be helping her out, not trying to get in her pants.

"Jaxson?"

"Oh, sorry." I hadn't heard what she'd said after asking about a bar.

"It's fine," she said and waved her hand dismissively. "We should head back to the cabin and hook up the fridge to your generator. Assuming you don't mind me borrowing it. I promise it's just until I get a job and can buy my own."

My cell phone buzzed in my pocket. I reached into my pants and grabbed my phone, holding out a finger to her to wait a second. It was Declan. "Hey, what's up?" I asked.

He had promised to tow her car for me, and while he was supposed to be at Eagle Tactical this afternoon, I hadn't heard about any big calls or operations coming through.

Usually, the team texted me if something important was going on, a big client, or a dangerous mission if I wasn't at the office.

"I pulled your girl's car from the ravine. Her tires are completely bald. The window was smashed, and the bumper dented. The bumper isn't a big deal, but the trunk was crushed and the latch is broken and won't be fixable. It'll cost her a few grand to make the car drivable, and that doesn't include getting it in shape for Breckenridge winter. What do you want me to do?"

I exhaled a heavy sigh. Ariella would not be happy about the news. Already, the smile fell from her face as I stared at her, like she already knew.

"Let me call you back," I said to Declan before hanging up. "Do you have full liability on your car?" I asked Ariella.

Wordlessly, she shook her head. I already suspected that was the case. "Declan says it'll be several grand,

and that doesn't get your car into safe shape for getting up the mountain. We can find you a set of used chains, but I'm not crazy about you driving up in that car. You need four-wheel drive or at least all-wheel drive on a vehicle if you're going to be working in another town and having to travel up and down the mountain pass daily."

"Shit," she said under her breath.

"Shit. Shit. Shit," Isabella repeated, staring at Ariella.

CHAPTER SEVEN

ARIELLA

I couldn't afford several grand in repairs on my car, let alone a new fridge. "Any chance there's a bus that'll take me to town?"

Should I just abandon the car? That's all it was good for anyhow.

Besides, my past was tied to that vehicle. Wasn't it better if I left it and every part of New York behind?

"There aren't any buses in Breckenridge, but I'm sure we can find you someone who can give you a lift who lives in town and works in the city."

"You guys consider where we were today a city?"

The population had been less than 10,000 people. It is hardly classified as a city.

We headed out of the booth at Lumberjack Shack and back to Jaxson's truck. He had started the engine and warmed up the vehicle for us before we got back inside.

I climbed into the passenger side and waited while he secured Isabella into the car seat.

He seemed like a pro, knowing exactly what to do in the least amount of time possible so that he could climb into the truck quickly. "You're good at that," I said.

It was a stupid comment to make, but I was impressed. My sister had two kids, and when she was pregnant with the second and in labor at the hospital, I was delegated to watching the littlest boy. It had taken me an hour to get him in his car seat, and even then, I wasn't comfortable with how it had been latched. It didn't seem secure.

"Thanks," he said as he climbed into the driver's seat.

Slamming the door shut, he put the truck into reverse before pulling out of the parking lot and onto the main road.

"Next stop, your house, to drop off the fridge. You're going to need groceries too, but that can wait."

"It can?" I was almost relieved by his suggestion to wait.

"Yes. We're going to need to chop up firewood before nightfall. Remember, you burned up everything dry and in the house."

"Can't I order some and have it delivered?"

"Sure, but it's not cheap," Jaxson said.

I knew that, but I was not an outdoorsy girl who chopped firewood.

I didn't know the next thing about splitting wood, and I wasn't incredibly strong, either. I wasn't expecting Jaxson to do it for me. I just thought the house wouldn't require firewood to keep warm.

I needed to stop blaming Mason for the listing. I should have come to Breckenridge and visited the cabin before paying for it with every dollar to my name.

"Daddy!" Isabella squealed from the backseat.

"Yes, sweetie?"

"I'm bored," she announced, whining and groaning as she tried to free herself from her car seat. Thankfully, it appeared too tight for her to unbuckle herself.

I turned around and offered her my undivided attention while Jaxson focused on the narrow, snow-covered road. It seemed the roads stayed covered with snow all winter, and it wasn't even the coldest months of the year.

"What's your favorite color?" I quizzed her, trying to keep her preoccupied for the rest of the drive.

"Purple," she squealed with delight and grinned proudly, her nose scrunched up. Her hands stalled on her buckle, already forgetting what she had been attempting to do. "You?"

"That's a tough one," I said. "I'd have to go with turquoise that shimmers, like a mermaid's tail."

"You're very specific," Jaxson said while he kept his focus on the road.

While I was turned to face Isabella, the car veered off the main road and up the long narrow driveway to my house. We were almost back.

"I like mermaids too!" Isabella squealed and clapped her hands together.

"You do?" It had been fairly obvious with her mermaid shirt, hairbow, and sneakers. "I never would have guessed it."

He pulled up to the front of the cabin and parked the truck. "Thank you." He kept his voice low and soft, and I wasn't sure if he was trying to keep Isabella from hearing or it was supposed to be a private moment between us.

I shifted in the front seat and brushed against his coat. "It's my pleasure," I said. After all, he'd done to help me, and we barely knew one another, it was the least I could do.

He shut off the truck and stepped out into the cold before unbuckling Isabella and carrying her on his hip.

I hurried to the front door, unlocked the entrance and gestured for him to bring his daughter inside. While it wasn't nearly as warm as it had been that morning, the house was still considerably comfortable.

The temperature would drop tonight. Leaving the door open to bring in the refrigerator would also cool the place.

"Izzie, you stay in here," he said, plopping her down on the sofa.

"But, Daddy, I want to be with you and Ella," she said, struggling to pronounce my name. It was sweet, endearing, really.

He bent down, crouched at her level, unbuttoning her jacket and sliding it off her shoulders. "Ariella," Jaxson said, correcting her as he slowly annunciated my name for her to repeat.

The little girl rolled her eyes at her daddy. "Ella. 'Tis what I said."

"It's all right," I said, resting a gentle hand on Jaxson's shoulder.

He stood and I took a step back, making room. There wasn't much space between the sofa and the coffee table for the two of us with Isabella on the couch. "Izzie, I need you to stay on the sofa, okay?"

"Yes, bossy Daddy," Isabella said.

"I'm telling you, I'm raising a teenage daughter already." Jaxson gestured for me to follow him outside. "Do you think you can give me a hand with the fridge, or is it too much for you to do?"

I may not have been as strong as Jaxson, but I didn't want to be forced to sit on the couch and watch. "I can help."

"Okay, good." He undid the ropes, and together we guided the fridge out of the truck and into the house.

Jaxson did most of the lifting and heavy work. I guided the fridge and made sure it didn't crush him.

Twenty minutes from start to finish, the fridge was in the kitchen, and the electric cord was left accessible for when the generator was brought over.

"Thank you again for everything." I hated being in his debt, but twice, he'd helped me, and I would not forget it.

"Don't mention it. I'm going to wheel the generator over. Can you stay here and keep an eye on Izzie?"

"Sure." I didn't know the first thing about kids.

She sat on the couch, her feet kicking the air, probably trying to reach the coffee table, but her legs were too short. He wouldn't be gone that long.

He slipped out the front door and left his truck. I frowned, watching from the window, curious why he didn't bring his vehicle with him.

"Where did Daddy go?" Isabella asked.

"He'll be right back." My stomach tensed. I could not deal with a crying toddler.

I dashed over to the sofa to sit beside her, attempting another distraction to keep her from growing upset. While I wanted to know if there was a girlfriend or partner in the picture, I wasn't sure how to delicately ask a three-year-old that question.

"What's your favorite thing to do with your Daddy?"

"Tickle fight!" she proclaimed and stood on my sofa, lifting her shirt to show me her belly.

"Do you want me to tickle you?" I asked her.

Isabella grinned and vigorously nodded her head. My fingers pretended to tickle her, but I didn't even come close to touch her before she squealed and giggled, jumping back.

"Oh, come on. That didn't tickle!" She'd make a superb actress someday. Jaxson was right about her practically being a teenager, being melodramatic.

"Tickle!" she squealed and tried to tickle my neck. Her fingers were chilly and wiggling, but it wasn't the least bit causing me to laugh.

I pretended to giggle and tickled her hips, and she squirmed with actual fits of giggles. Her legs kicked, and her chin bent downward as she squealed with delight.

I let go for a second, allowing her to catch her breath. I didn't want her in tears or upset.

"More!" she leaped into my arms. "Tickle more!"

I tickled her a little more, watching her thrash as she giggled, her cheeks rosy.

"Does your daddy have a girlfriend?" I asked, not entirely sure she could answer between her fits of laughter. I probably shouldn't have been asking about him, but I couldn't stop myself, the curiosity getting the better of me.

"Daddy likes to play with the boys." She giggled and slipped from my grasp. My hands paused.

"Oh." That wasn't what I expected to hear. While I shouldn't have been disappointed, my heart sunk like an anvil in the sea.

Jaxson stalked into the house, an extra pair of boots in hand. "What's that you're telling about me, Izzie?"

She snuck away from me, climbed off the sofa, and ran toward her daddy. "You like to play with Declan and Aiden."

CHAPTER EIGHT

JAXSON

Shit.

Was my daughter telling Ariella I was gay?

I was pretty confident Izzie didn't even know what that meant, let alone what she was saying. I liked women a lot.

While I didn't bring women around because of Izzie, that didn't mean I didn't enjoy their company.

I put the winter boots down on the ground and bent down to Izzie's level, hugging her. "I work with Declan and Aiden, Izzie. I don't think the right term is playing with them."

Isabella's brow furrowed. She had no idea what I was saying, and it didn't matter.

I glanced back at Ariella on the sofa and hoped she understood.

"I brought you these," I said, showing her the fur-lined boots.

They'd been a gift I hadn't given that sat in the back of my closet, unopened and unworn.

"I hope they'll fit, I'm not sure what size you are, and I don't have a lot of spare women's boots lying around."

I handed her the shoes, and she slipped them on to see how well they fit.

"I must be Cinderella," she joked and wiggled her feet. "These are super comfy. I will not ask why they were at your house. I honestly don't care. I'm just glad to have a warm pair of boots again, and I promise to return them as soon as I get mine from the car."

"Don't worry about it. They won't be missed," I said.

"Where's the generator?" Ariella asked.

I pointed toward the window on the opposite side of the cabin.

"Around back. It needs to stay outside, but I'm going to hook up an extension cord and run it out the back door. I'll tape the cord down if I need to, to make sure you can shut the door tight."

"Thank you," she said and stood, coming toward me. "Can I help with anything?"

"You've helped enough." I didn't intend to come across as harsh, but it was clear she was asking Izzie about me. Why else was my daughter telling her I liked to play with boys?

I scratched the back of my neck and headed over to the fridge, hooking up the extension cord before taking it outside.

Ariella stood in the hallway watching me.

"I'm sorry if I was out of line." She kept her voice down so that only I could hear her, which I appreciated immensely. I didn't want Izzie to have a plethora of questions later.

"Next time, if you want to know something, just ask me."

"Right. I'll do that," she said and pursed her lips.

Already, I could tell she wanted to ask me something, but I wasn't sure what it was. Had she asked Izzie while I'd been outside and hadn't gotten the answer she hoped for? Why was she asking twenty questions about me?

"You're staring," I said as I stepped outside. She hung in the doorframe, keeping the back door open while watching me hook up the generator outside and start the engine on it.

"Just watching you work," Ariella said.

There was more to it than that, but I wasn't sure what she was getting at. "Listen, I like women. I just try to keep my daughter away from anyone I date."

Why was I telling her this? She hadn't asked. She was probably just being friendly with Izzie, and I got the wrong impression from what I'd heard when coming into the cabin.

"Is Isabella's mom in the picture?" she asked, leaning against the doorframe.

She wrapped her arms around herself, her jacket abandoned inside the house.

Ariella had to be freezing. I hurried up with the generator and ushered her back inside, where it was warmer.

"No, she's not. It's just the two of us." I didn't elaborate, not because I didn't want to, but because we were back inside, and Izzie was within earshot.

I didn't want her to overhear the conversation.

"I'm happy to talk about it with you, but it would be better if we had that discussion when it's just the two of us."

"Of course," she said.

I shut the door and locked it, the electric cord pushed to the side. "I'll secure the cord next time I come by."

I could tape it down, but I needed to get some tape and didn't have any on hand with me at the moment. I knew what was in the cabin, and I hadn't left any behind.

"I'm sure it'll be fine. Thank you again for all your help today, and I will pay you back for everything," Ariella said.

I wasn't worried about the money, whether she was good for it. That was beside the point. It was clear she was in a bind and needed help.

I hadn't made her life any easier with the property listing, and guilt weighed heavily on me. Even though it hadn't been intentional, it still was clear that she struggled to make ends meet.

I dug my hand into my coat pocket, almost forgetting the other device I'd brought over from my house.

"For your cell phone," I said, retrieving a small solar powered charging device. "It doesn't need outside light. You can put it on a windowsill."

I took a few steps into the kitchen and set up the device with the solar panel facing the window, keeping it on the ledge inside above the sink.

"Do you have your phone handy?" I wanted to make sure it was set up before I left.

She headed toward her bed and retrieved her knapsack that sat on the bottom shelf of the end table. Crouched down, she dug through the bag for a moment before finding her cell phone.

I hadn't seen a flip phone in ages, especially with the craze for smartphones.

"Wow. You keep it old school," I said, taking the device from her before plugging it into the solar charger.

"I'm all about practicality and what I need. Well, that or you can consider me cheap." She flashed me a wide grin.

She was hiding something, but I couldn't be certain what it was.

"Thank you for the charger. I should call my sister once my phone is charged. I'm sure she's wondering if I made it here safely."

Everyone I knew had a smartphone, and anyone with a burner style flip phone in my line of business usually had secrets. I tried not to let the nagging suspicion cloud my judgment.

"You're welcome to use my phone," I said, pulling it out from my pants pocket.

"That isn't necessary." She waved her hand dismissively. "It can wait until tonight. I'm sure the phone will have enough of a charge before nightfall.

I hope, anyway."

It would take a few hours to charge the battery, but it would be usable within the hour. The solar charger was top of the line commercial grade used by our team. It wasn't something you could pick up off the shelf of a store. I had used it countless times on Eagle Tactical missions when I was in the field and didn't have easy access to an accessible outlet.

"Use my phone," I insisted and pushed my phone at her.

She glanced over at the device. Her tongue darted out to the corner of her lips.

Was she debating whether to call her sister in front of me? Had she wanted the call to be private, and I had overstepped her boundaries? She didn't say a word, just held the phone in her hand.

"I can sit with Izzie and give you some privacy."

There wasn't a ton of privacy in the cabin. It was one large room, like a studio style setup.

"It's not that. I don't have her phone number memorized," she said, her cheeks red.

Was she embarrassed about not knowing the number offhand? I could recant every phone number for my military buddies, they were like family to me.

Had her sister's number recently changed, and she hadn't had time to memorize it?

She handed me back my cell phone. "I'm sure she can wait a few more hours. It's only been a day." Ariella didn't sound the least bit concerned about calling her sister later.

I held my tongue, not wanting to make a scene. If she didn't remember the number, there were ways I could help, I had resources and connections through Eagle Tactical, but I wasn't sure that was what she wanted. I didn't want to push her and make her uncomfortable.

"If it were someone I cared about and hadn't heard from them, I'd be concerned," I said.

I didn't elaborate that I'd probably have unleashed the entire task force of Eagle Tactical to go looking for that person. We were different. She had moved to the middle of nowhere, with no connections. Was it possible she and her sister weren't close?

"Daddy, I have to go potty!" Izzie squealed from the sofa and stood on the couch cushions.

I shot her a look of warning that she'd better sit her butt down or stand on the floor. Isabella knew that jumping on beds and couches was not allowed.

The little tyrant did whatever she damned well pleased half the time, though. Being a single dad wasn't easy.

"I think that's my cue to take her home," I said.

"She can use the bathroom here," Ariella offered. "I have indoor plumbing."

"You're welcome for that," I half-joked. I had been responsible, along with my military buddies, for setting up indoor plumbing. While we hooked up the indoor plumbing and PVC inside and under the floorboards, we'd also hired a licensed plumber who doubled as an excavator to hook up to the sewer line.

"I'm going to take her back home, let her use the little kid potty, and then put her down for a nap."

"No nap!" Izzie exclaimed, jumping on the sofa.

"Sit your butt down!" I scolded her. She knew better and was testing my limits or showing off for Ariella. Perhaps it was a bit of both.

Pretty soon, she'd meltdown without an afternoon nap. It was only a matter of time. She'd done well today, but I couldn't depend on her lasting through dinner.

Izzie went from a standing position on the sofa to jumping into a sitting position. "Potty, Daddy!"

"Do you mind if we use your bathroom?"

Izzie followed me to the small private bathroom, and I helped her before she climbed off the toilet and ran past me with her pants down.

"Oh, my gosh. You, child, will be the death of me," I muttered, flushing the toilet before washing my hands.

I stepped out of the bathroom, and Ariella was bent down to Izzie's level, helping her pull her pants back up. *Thank you*, I mouthed to her.

She smiled and nodded.

"Come on, Izzie." I grabbed her coat and helped her get her arms into the sleeves while she thrashed about, not wanting to go home.

"No nap!" she squealed.

I groaned and tried to control my temper. Isabella was tired, and I hadn't kept to her routine. It was my fault she was behaving like a rambunctious toddler. "We need to leave Ariella here. Say goodbye."

I slid one arm into her sleeve and worked on the other one before she slid her arm back out.

"I don't mean to interrupt. I'm sure you have this handled, but she could nap on my bed," Ariella offered.

I shot a glance at her over my shoulder.

"I mean, I need to learn to chop firewood. If you don't mind giving me a hand, she could stay inside and nap in my bed," she repeated.

It wasn't the worst idea, and Izzie seemed to go for it, nodding vigorously with bright, wide, doe-like eyes.

"That still means you need a nap, little miss," I said, pointing at Izzie.

She slipped her coat off, scooted past me, and ran for the queen-sized mattress. I tucked her under the covers while Ariella closed the curtains, making the cabin darker. Quietly, I headed to the front door and waited for Ariella to put her coat and shoes on.

A few minutes later, we were outside, just the two of us.

"I'm sorry if I overstepped," Ariella said, quick to apologize. "I know you have a routine, and I just thought I might help." She looked flustered and nervous. Was she worried I'd yell at her?

I exhaled a long, heavy breath I hadn't realized I'd been holding. "It's fine. Izzie tends to meltdown when she doesn't get her afternoon nap, and half the time, she fights with me about lying down. If she doesn't rest, she's crabby for dinner and sometimes falls asleep before she eats. It's just a vicious cycle. Thank you for offering her your bed. She likes you."

"I like her too. She's a good kid."

It was obvious Izzie had already grown attached to Ariella. It had only been a day together, and I had seen the sparkle in Izzie's eye, the smile that adorned her face when she looked at Ariella.

There hadn't been a female figure in Isabella's life. That had been my fault. The guys were great, helping look after her and support me, but it wasn't a woman figure.

One day, she'd need someone to come to and talk with about things that she didn't want to discuss with her dad. I had thought I had another ten years, but that glint in Izzie's eyes told me more than her words at this point could ever do.

I slid my gloves on as we stood outside on the porch. "You have a shed around back," I said, changing the subject. "There's an ax inside to chop wood, and around back is a stump where you can do the chopping."

"Great." Her voice dripped with sarcasm. Her tongue darted out past her cherry red lips before chewing on her bottom lip. "Any chance I can find wood in the forest and skip the chopping part?"

"Wouldn't that be nice? There are probably some logs, and I'm not suggesting you go all lumberjack style and chop down a tree, but you might come across logs that are too big to fit into your wood-burning stove. You'll need to know how to size those logs properly, which involves using an ax," I said.

She followed me as I headed around to the shed and opened the doors. I retrieved an ax from inside, sheltered from the snow, and then shut the doors when I was done, to keep the contents inside dry.

"There's an ATV in the shed. It's old and dated, but it works. It should help you get around the woods and into town if you follow the trail with the orange triangles." I pointed toward the entrance to the trail on her property. It followed along the riverbed and was a shortcut to town.

"That's great. Thanks," she said.

Ariella watched as I grabbed a log and placed it on the large stump, preparing to split it.

I pulled back the ax and swung; it split cleanly into two pieces. I wasn't sure how to explain the action. It was easier to show her. "Piece of cake. Your turn," I said, handing her the handle of the ax, the blade toward the ground.

"Right." She took the ax, and I grabbed a log and situated it on the stump before I took a step back to give her space. She gripped the handle with two hands and swung back before following through, going forward in one swift motion.

She got the ax's blade a few inches into the piece of wood before it got stuck. "It won't budge. I think I broke it."

"It's not broken. You just have to dislodge it," I said, taking the ax and lifting the blade, hitting it sideways against the stump. It took a half swing, nothing too forceful to break it free.

"Are you sure I can't just gather firewood in the forest?" she asked with a half-hearted laugh. The smile on her face was gone, and the glint in her eyes had faded. "I think I may have oversold the idea of living in a small town in the mountains."

"You'll get the hang of it," I said, hoping to boost her confidence.

I didn't imagine it was easy for her, moving out into the middle of nowhere. While I was curious about her reasons, I wasn't one to push.

I certainly could have done a little research with the tools and resources from Eagle Tactical, but it didn't feel right. She wasn't Izzie's babysitter. Had that been the case, I would have run her name through the database and dug through her past to make sure Izzie was safe.

"Hopefully before summer," she said with a hearty laugh.

My phone buzzed in my pocket, and I pulled out my cell phone and removed my gloves so I could answer. "Eagle Tactical, this is Jaxson," I said, taking a step back from the stump to allow for a little privacy. I could tell from the caller I.D. that someone was calling about the business, and it wasn't a personal call.

"Hi, Jaxson. This is Bridget Sanders from the Blue Sky Resort. We wanted to get a background check run for a new hire. Is that something you guys can do for us this week?"

"Yes. If you want to email me the form with the employee's name and information, I can have one of our guys run the background check and get it back to you shortly."

I gave her my email address before I hung up the phone and headed back toward Ariella as she split another piece of wood in half.

I hoped she was the new hire the background check was for. Knowing that I'd be the one running the information on her past and digging up all her dirty little secrets, I was covered in filth.

CHAPTER NINE

ARIELLA

"Everything okay?" I asked.

He'd gotten a work call, and while he'd taken a step away to answer it privately, I couldn't help but wonder who it was or what he might need to do.

Eagle Tactical.

He'd mentioned the name of the company.

While I hadn't heard of them before arriving in Breckenridge, the fact he worked there had me curious, especially when he'd told me former military soldiers owned the company.

"Just a work thing," he said and shoved his phone back into his pocket.

Was he hiding something? Could he not talk about work? A part of me was curious about what he did for a living, how he coped with danger.

"Do you need to go to work?" I asked. I didn't know what his hours were. Just because I didn't have a job, didn't mean he didn't have to work.

"No, I have the day off," Jaxson said, matter of factly.

He stepped closer toward me and took a breath, a pause before coming up from behind. His hand rested on my hip. I expelled a soft, nervous breath when he rested his hands over mine to help guide me with the ax.

The moment was intimate, and had it not been so cold outside, I might have been warmer, but the truth was my fingers were numb, and my face tingled. Even with my gloves, hat, boots, and thick winter coat, I was still cold.

"You're freezing," Jaxson said, his breath against my cheek.

I didn't hide it from him. "Yes. I hate the cold."

He laughed and pulled me closer, the ax fumbling from our hands to the ground. "Careful," he warned me. "You could get hurt dropping a blade so carelessly."

We'd both dropped it without thinking, but I didn't want to point that out.

I spun around in his embrace, our jackets thick and keeping me from really feeling his body against mine like I wanted.

He reached for my hat and pulled it down a little farther on my head to cover me a little better. "We should go inside and warm up," Jaxson said.

"I don't want to wake Izzie."

"That kid will sleep through anything," Jaxson said, his breath warm against my frozen cheeks. He took my gloved hand and led me back into the cabin. The warmth of the house immediately put me at ease, and while it wasn't as toasty as it had been earlier, Jaxson brought a few logs inside and brought the fire roaring back to life. "Do you know how to start a fire?" he asked.

I removed my cold, damp outdoor clothes—my hat, gloves, shoes, and jacket—leaving them by the fire to dry.

"If I have lighter fluid and a long lighter, I can figure it out."

"You are not using lighter fluid in your wood-burning stove. Is that clear?" His tone forceful and his eyebrows raised in alarm, he didn't seem the least bit amused in my humor.

"That was a joke." It was mostly a joke. I'd had bonfires outside and knew how to start those types of fires.

He loaded the wood into the stove, and the hot ashes at the bottom caught right away. Another few minutes and the fire roared back to life.

I sat quietly on the sofa, and Jaxson came over once he seemed satisfied with the fire, sitting beside me. We'd only known one another two days. I wasn't ready for a relationship, even with the most handsome man I'd ever met.

If there hadn't been a kid involved, I would have let my guard down further and allowed myself to indulge in a fantasy involving him, but that was out of the question. We couldn't, and besides, I wasn't exactly sure what was going on with Izzie's mother.

"You're quiet," Jaxson said, sitting back relaxing on the sofa.

"Just thinking," I said, avoiding his stare as he kept watching me.

"About?"

"It's been a long time since I've been around another man." I wasn't sure I should have brought up my ex-husband or the divorce, but it was the truth.

I wasn't used to dating or sex with anyone but the bastard I'd been married to for way too long. There was more to it, a place I didn't want to go or drudge up. Not that he would have known.

Jaxson sighed, running a hand through his hair. "I know the feeling. Well, maybe not another man." Chuckling, he nudged me. "Have you ever been married?"

"Yes." I glanced at Jaxson, exhaling a heavy breath. "We're not together anymore. He's a distant memory, one I wish I could erase."

"Divorced or separated?" he asked.

"Divorced. What about you?" I held my tongue on the fact he was in prison. I wasn't ready to talk about that with anyone.

"I've never been married. After I took full custody of Izzie, she's been my entire life."

I brushed a strand of hair behind my ear. The way he stared at me sent a shiver through my body and made my insides toasty.

"I can see that. It's clear you're a good father."

"Thank you," Jaxson said, his eyes shining.

"It's true." I shifted on the sofa and our legs touched briefly.

"I have to ask, and I hope you don't mind, but many people who come out to the mountains, a small town in the middle of nowhere, are running from something or someone. Are you running, Ariella?"

The way he said my name made me shiver.

Could he know my secrets? Did he know who I was and what I'd been accused of doing?

I hadn't changed my first name, and Ariella wasn't the most common name, like Mary or Jennifer. I assumed hiding in plain sight had been to my advantage, but I was wrong.

CHAPTER TEN

JAXSON

"No," she whispered, her gaze meeting mine, our eyes locked.

I tried reading her expression, watching her face and body language to determine if she was lying to me. I'd been around enough interrogations in the military on both sides of them that I could see right through a liar.

What was she hiding?

Did it have more to do with her past and ex-husband than anything else? I didn't want to hound her with questions or run a background check on her solely out of my curiosity. It was wrong, and I didn't want to be that person, questioning her every move, not trusting her.

Though I had to remember, we barely knew one another.

I wanted to get to know her.

There weren't many women who were single in Breckenridge, and the ones who were, I knew all of them. Some had approached me, asked me out, or pursued me countless times. I had turned them down, and it had grown easier once Izzie was in the picture.

"You're just starting over?" I offered in the way of an explanation.

"That's right," she said as relief flooded her features. Her shoulders relaxed, and her eyes were no longer doe-like.

She was hiding something. I should have afforded Ariella her privacy and secrets, but I couldn't protect her if I didn't know what was going on.

Was I overreacting because of my line of work and she didn't need protection?

I'd seen it all before, women in abusive marriages fleeing their husbands. That had been my first fleeting thought when she'd told me she'd been married and had come out here to live. I suspected there was more to it than that.

"Well, I'm glad you picked this cabin," I said, stretching my arms before turning my gaze toward the ceiling and then back to her. "It's nice to have a neighbor who isn't Mason."

"No kidding," she laughed under her breath. "How do you work with him?"

"He's a good guy," I said. "Albeit a pain in the ass, but he's got his heart in the right place, and he always has my back."

The longer I stared at her, the more I wanted to kiss her.

It had been three years of focusing on Izzie and not allowing myself the opportunity to indulge in my desires. I didn't want to ruin a perfectly good friendship that we'd already established, but was it worth it?

My heart constricted, but my body leaned forward, my lips closing in but pausing, waiting for her to make the next move to lean into me.

Her breath hovered over my lips, the warmth of her mouth teasing me, making my body ache for her touch.

My heart pounded against my ribcage as my lips parted slightly. I shifted closer if that was possible, without pulling her into my lap.

Her eyes lowered to my lips. The cabin warmed as I slid my hand to the back of her neck. My fingers played with her hair, letting the moment drag on, our lips not quite touching yet.

Ariella's lips parted, and a jolt of electricity coursed through my body as she leaned in, brushing her lips against mine.

Starving for her touch, I pulled her closer, one hand at the back of her neck, the other on her lower back. I wanted our bodies to melt together, to become one.

She moaned, and I took the opportunity as an encouragement to continue.

I pulled her into my lap, her hips against mine, our lips fused with a heated passion. I wanted nothing more than to strip her naked and drive myself into her, but I couldn't do that. I wouldn't do that, not with Izzie in the room.

This would have to satisfy the urgent need building within my body.

"Jaxson," she gasped and pulled back, her breath ragged. Her forehead rested against mine, and she was panting hard.

My eyes shut, enjoying the moment and the intimacy between us. I hadn't realized how much I missed being this close to someone.

"We need to take things slow," Ariella said.

I knew she was right, we'd just met, and I had my daughter to think of foremost. "Yes, slow is good." I didn't want to lie, but kissing her had unleashed a flurry of emotions pent up for the past three years.

I wanted to carry her to my bed and ravish her, but she was right.

"Slow is overrated," she whispered and pressed her lips firmly against mine.

I moaned, my body responding to her touch, her kisses, the way she whispered. Everything inside me was on fire. Her hips shifted and thrust against me.

I groaned; she was killing me. I wouldn't be able to keep any measure of self-control if she continued the ministrations against my crotch.

"Ariella," I rasped, trying to regain my strength to stop what we'd both started before it was too late. "Slow," I said, trying to remind her of her earlier words. It was hard to say more than one word at a time.

My brain wasn't working, my body fueled with a desire for her.

"Sorry," she whispered and climbed off my body. Had she realized what she'd done to me? Could she feel the evidence of my desire for her?

She sat on the sofa, turned to face me. Her fingers rested on her thighs.

"I think we should go slow. You have a daughter who needs your undivided attention, and I—"

"You, what?" I asked, wanting her to be honest and open with me. I pushed an errant strand of hair behind her ear and waited for her to answer my question.

"I'm not ready to trust again, to be in a relationship. I have a feeling you're not looking for a one-night stand, and that's all I can offer you."

My stomach knotted, and I scooted back. Her words burned my heart.

Is that what she wanted?

I wasn't interested in sleeping with random women or even a friends-with-benefits scenario. I had a daughter, and anyone I brought around, I wanted for the long run, not for one night.

While I didn't know how long she'd been divorced, we had just met. I needed to give her time. She was right. We needed to slow down, take a break from whatever was happening between us.

"You're right, I'm not interested in an empty fuck," I said and stood.

Staying the afternoon, letting Izzie have a nap, it was all a mistake.

I laced my boots and grabbed my coat. I didn't want to wake Isabella, but I could quietly put her jacket on her and put her into the car seat. If I was lucky, the short drive back to the cabin would lull her to sleep, and she could finish her nap at home.

CHAPTER ELEVEN

ARIELLA

My lips still tingled from the recent kiss.

When I'd told him I wanted to go slow, he seemed onboard with the idea. I hadn't intended to hurt him, but I needed to be honest.

I wasn't ready for a commitment, and I suspected he wanted a wife. He had a daughter and was probably looking to finish his family.

I wasn't sure I could be that for him, ever.

I sat on the sofa, lost and flustered as he gathered his coat and boots. "You don't have to go."

"Yes, I do." He zipped his jacket, put his beanie back on, and then secured Isabella's jacket around her little body before carrying her to the door. "I'll call Declan and have him give you a ride to pick up your car when it's done at the shop."

Great.

Now he didn't want to see me again.

"Okay. Thank you." I stood and headed toward the kitchen to check my cell phone that sat on the windowsill. The battery had just about fully charged.

I unplugged his solar charger. "Here, take this." He wouldn't be back for it, and I wasn't sure I wanted to face him again, either.

"I'll give you my number. Text me, so I have your number, and I can forward it to Declan."

"Okay." I punched in his digits and texted him. *It's Ariella.* I didn't send anything special. I didn't know what to say. The heated moment between us had turned as cold as ice.

I'd really screwed up.

"I'll see you around," Jaxson said and headed with Izzie to the truck.

I watched from the door. I stood awkwardly with my arms crossed in front of me. The chilly wind made me numb.

He backed out of the driveway, and I shut the door.

How was I going to make this right? Could I fix what I'd done?

He didn't know my secrets, that Ben had stolen millions from investors in a Ponzi scheme, and we both had been charged with dozens of crimes. He'd been convicted of several felonies. I'd stood trial, and while I'd gotten off with no convictions, I had been threatened countless times back in New York. That had been one reason why I'd left.

I wanted what happened to be forever in the past, buried. I had done nothing wrong. I didn't know what he'd done, but my name had been on the company papers because we were married.

I'd signed forms I didn't understand, and that made me an accessory. I should have been more careful, but I trusted him. I wasn't involved with the company. I never saw the financial records or accounts. That had been how I'd been able to get off without a single conviction.

I truly was clueless.

"I'm sorry," I whispered to the chilly afternoon air as Jaxson had already pulled away and down the road out of sight. I hadn't meant to hurt him. I didn't want him to think less of me or blame me, like every one of Ben's investors had.

While I hadn't been convicted, I still held the weight of guilt, dirty of his crimes. I should have known what was going on.

My eyes burned with tears.

The only person I'd gotten close to since my divorce and the trial, and he knew nothing of my past. I'd ruined my clean slate without him even knowing the truth.

Should I have leaped in heart first and taken a chance with Jaxson?

I couldn't lie to him. After everything he'd done for me, I would not hurt him. At least that hadn't been my intention.

With a resigned sigh, I dialed my sister, Delphine. I wasn't expecting a warm greeting, but she had insisted I call her when I got settled in my new home.

"Hello?" Delphine's soft voice resounded through the phone.

"Hey, Delphine, it's me, Ariella." I paused, unsure what to say. We hadn't been close in years.

She blamed me for what happened with Ben.

When I was charged and searching for a lawyer, she'd shut me out and told me she wanted nothing to do with me. I wasn't looking for a handout or a free pass. I just needed help, and she turned her back on me.

She was a paralegal and knew plenty of defense attorneys but didn't want any association with me. I hated her for that year, but then I saw her at the trial when I was put on the stand. She'd been in the back row.

That had been the beginning of our reconciliation.

"Hey," her voice was soft, and her single word of greeting sounded hesitant.

"Is this a bad time?" I asked. I collapsed onto the sofa and stretched out my feet to rest on the coffee table.

"It's never a great time," Delphine said.

"Right." Why was I bothering to call her when she wanted nothing to do with me? "Well, you said to let you know when I got my feet planted in Breckenridge. I'm here. Everything is great." I gritted my teeth.

When we were younger, she could see right through my lies. Had that changed?

"Good. Listen, Marcus is home. I can't talk right now." She kept her voice low, hardly above a whisper. Marcus hated me, and she wasn't telling him I called. I'd have done the same had the situation been reversed.

Marcus was her husband of ten years. He was the king of assholes, well, maybe the prince. He narrowly was behind Benjamin, and while Marcus hadn't cheated on Delphine or stolen millions from his clients, he was more than just a bit of a snob. He acted like he was untouchable and could do no wrong.

"Okay. Bye," I said and hung up the phone. I don't know why I bothered. While I was expecting a frosty greeting, a part of me hoped we could reconnect. I couldn't have been more wrong.

Ending the call, I glanced down at the missed voicemail and hit play.

"Hi, Ms. Cole, this is Bridget Sanders with Blue Sky Resort. We met yesterday at my office. We'd like to formally offer you the flex position. We wanted to let you know that we've started the background check, and assuming everything goes smoothly, we'd like you to start first thing Monday morning. Please call us back if you have any questions. Otherwise, we'll be in touch with you later this week."

I hung up the phone, my stomach in knots, waiting to hear if I'd cleared the background check.

I texted Jaxson.

He probably didn't want to hear from me, but I didn't want him worrying about me and getting food for dinner or groceries.

If the ATV in the shed could get me into town, I could take my backpack and get some food for the house. While I had little money, I had a credit card that would have to suffice.

Thanks for the help today and for everything. Taking the ATV out to the store. I texted.

Remember to stay on the orange triangle trail. Be careful.

CHAPTER TWELVE

JAXSON

Early the next morning, I headed into Eagle Tactical after I dropped Izzie off at daycare. I had avoided my work emails, which meant I needed to open up the correspondence from Blue Sky Resort.

Lucy sat at the front desk, a cup of coffee in hand.

"Good morning," I said as I passed her desk and headed for my office.

"Fridays are wonderful," Lucy said, sipping her coffee.

Sitting down, I jiggled the mouse and waited for the screen to light up. It was time to find out if Ariella got the job.

I shouldn't have cared one way or the other, but I did. I wanted her to be happy, and while I wasn't strapped for cash, I would eventually need my generator back, which meant she needed to purchase one.

I opened my emails and walked away from my desk long enough to grab myself a coffee while I let all the emails file into my inbox.

"Morning," Mason said. "How did things go with the spitfire?"

I grunted under my breath.

That was certainly one way to describe Ariella. I didn't think she was trouble other than the possibility that she very well might break my heart.

Spending the rest of the day apart yesterday had been a wise decision. I didn't want to get emotionally involved with someone who couldn't meet my needs.

I'd learned that about Emma. She had only been interested in one thing, sex, and while that had been fun, she wasn't interested in being a mother to our little girl.

"That good?" Mason asked. He stood by the coffeepot and poured himself a drink. I waited until he was done to do the same.

I didn't want to kiss and tell or speak ill of her. I had no reason to, and she had done nothing wrong. "Everything's fine. I dropped her off yesterday after loaning her my generator."

I didn't go into detail with Mason about purchasing her a fridge or teaching her to chop firewood. He'd give me crap, and I'd never hear the end.

His eyes narrowed as he studied me.

"You have the hots for the new girl," Mason crooned.

"Oh, shut it." I would not listen to his insistent teasing. Nothing happened as far as he knew.

I poured myself a cup of coffee and took it to my desk. I sat down and sipped my hot beverage, the blackness of the coffee fitting my mood.

Mason put down his coffee on the corner of my desk. He folded his arms across his chest and watched me.

"What is it?" I asked. Mason lingered until he got what he wanted, but there was nothing to tell. At least nothing I planned on sharing.

"Bridget Sanders called this morning and left two messages. She's anxious about the two new hires and getting backgrounds run ASAP."

I groaned and ran a hand through my hair. Background checks and research weren't the most exciting aspects of our job.

It was simple work, easy pay, and I should have been grateful for the extra income it brought into Eagle Tactical, but I preferred being out in the field.

"She called me yesterday on my day off. I told her to email me the paperwork, and I'd get to it as soon as I could." Bridget could wait a day or two for the background checks to come back.

Mason shifted to sit at the edge of my desk. "I think Bridget has a crush on you. Why else would she call your cell phone when she could have submitted the requests through regular channels?"

"You're crazy," I said. The woman was in her mid-sixties. She was nice, but she wasn't my type. I was pushing forty and preferred women closer to my age. "She's always been impatient, wanting results before she even sends over the employees' names."

"True." Mason pushed himself off my desk and retrieved his cup of coffee. "She copied me on the two hires. Did you see the names yet?"

Had that been why Mason was hanging around my desk and pestering me? "Let me guess, one of them is Ariella." I already knew she'd applied for the position at Blue Sky Resort. That would mean she should get the job, which was good news.

"Yes, and the other one is your least favorite person."

I had no clue who that could be. "My mother?" I joked.

"Wow. I'll remember to tell her that at the next holiday dinner I'm invited to," Mason said, his lips curved upwards. He nudged my shoulder. "Have a look."

I rolled my eyes before I found the email and opened up the application to read the individuals' names. The first application was Ariella Cole, that hadn't been a surprise. At least she'd get the job. I opened the second application and coughed, practically choking on air.

Mason smacked my back. "Don't die over it."

"Emma Foster." I read the name aloud. "What's she doing in Breckenridge?" I asked Mason, not that I should have expected him to know the answer.

My daughter's birth mother had returned.

"Beats me," Mason said. "I thought she lived in Los Angeles."

"So did I." That's where she lived three years ago when Izzie was born.

Mason sipped his coffee, his eyes on me the entire time. "You're pissed. I can see it all over your face."

"Well, I'm not happy that she's suddenly back in town. She gave up her rights to Izzie."

I hoped Emma hadn't changed her mind and now wanted to be part of the equation. That wasn't a possibility, not for me. I didn't want to confuse Isabella, either.

What if Emma left again? I had to protect my little girl, and if it meant keeping Emma away from Izzie, I would do whatever was necessary.

"You could make sure she doesn't get the job at Blue Sky Resort," Mason said. His eyes crinkled with a grin that lit up his face.

"You're absolutely mad if you think I'm going to manipulate the results of the background check."

That wasn't something I could do. Even if I didn't want Emma around, I would not destroy her life or her future. I reached for my coffee, taking another sip.

"Do you want me to do it?" Mason asked.

A part of me wanted him to do whatever was necessary to keep Emma away and Izzie safe, but I would never condone such an action or be involved in any part of it.

"You know I can't say yes." Even though a small piece of me wanted to ensure that Emma was gone from our lives.

"You should confront her head-on, not avoid the situation. If she's going to be working at Blue Sky Resort, go visit her," Mason said.

He stepped back from my desk and stalked toward the door.

"That's what I would do. Make it clear you want nothing to do with her, and if she plans on sticking around town, it won't be for Isabella or you."

I exhaled a heavy breath. Mason was right.

"Yeah, I can do that." I also had her temporary address on her background check application.

I glanced over the information. I recognized the address as a rental unit, a small cabin outside of town not too far from the resort. I could visit her and give her a heads up before investing any more time and energy into our community.

Whatever regrets she had about Izzie, it was too late. I would not let her hurt my daughter.

"Can you run the backgrounds while I stop over at Emma's house?"

"Sure thing," Mason said. "You know how much I love digging into people's lives and uncovering their dirt."

———————

I drove toward the Blue Sky Resort. Just across the street were log cabin rental properties. I pulled up out front of cabin #218 and climbed out of my truck.

Exhaling a heavy breath, my stomach in knots, I gave a forceful knock on the door. I didn't want to be here, but it had to be done. I would not let her interfere with my daughter.

The door creaked open sluggishly and in no rush. Standing in her silken negligee, one hand on the door, she glanced me over from head to toe. "Jaxson, I wasn't expecting to see you."

"Seriously? That's where you want to start."

I couldn't believe the nerve of her! I stomped past her front door, letting myself into the rental property. The cabin was small, much smaller than the place Ariella had purchased.

"What are you doing in town?" I asked, my voice booming. I didn't pretend to be thrilled to see her because I wasn't the least bit happy about her return.

Emma shut the door behind her and scampered into the room. "I'm applying for a job. By the looks of it, you already deduced that much. They must have asked Eagle Tactical to do the background check, am I right?"

"You shouldn't be here, Emma. You signed away your rights as Izzie's mother." I would not let her come running back into our lives and ruin everything.

She wrung her hands together in front of her. "I know, and I shouldn't have done that," she said, staring at me with her piercing brown eyes. "I wasn't ready to be a mother back then, but I am now."

"No." My answer was firm. "You planned on putting her up for adoption. Signing away your parental right to me is no different. You don't get to run off and then decide to come back and play parent when you feel like it."

Emma's eyes welled up. "Jaxson, please."

"No. I won't stand in the way of you taking this job, but you are not to have contact with my daughter." I headed for the door.

"Our daughter," she whispered.

My cell phone buzzed, and I took the moment as an opportunity to leave. I grabbed my phone and stepped outside of the cabin, shutting the door behind myself. I didn't want Emma hearing the conversation or her chasing after me. "Hey, Mason. What's up?" I recognized his number.

"You will not believe this, but Ariella Cole, she was married to Benjamin Ryan."

"The same Benjamin Ryan who went to prison for stealing millions from investors?"

This day just went from bad to worse.

My stomach dropped as my legs failed to cooperate, as though they were encased in lead. I approached my truck and climbed inside, sitting in the front seat, trying to regroup.

My head spun.

I knew a woman like Ariella didn't move out into the mountains in a small town in the middle of nowhere because she liked the outdoors. She wanted to get off-grid.

Had she played me for a fool with not having electricity? I'd have bet anything she didn't want electricity. She didn't want to be found.

"That's right. Her married name, Ariella Ryan, came up when I searched, but her records were expunged. I did a little further digging when I recognized her name and the name of her ex-husband. She was arrested and charged but acquitted in a court of law," Mason said. "As far as her past is concerned, she's clean enough to get the job, but I thought you might want to know."

"Fuck."

I'd lost a pretty penny with her husband. The money that I believed I'd invested into real estate had instead been used in a Ponzi scheme, using my cash to pay other investors, until he'd gotten caught.

My entire life savings had vanished one day, and while Benjamin had gone to prison, I didn't believe Ariella was as innocent as she pretended to be.

CHAPTER THIRTEEN

ARIELLA

A loud, forceful knock pounded against my front door. I wasn't expecting visitors.

"Just a sec!" I called, coming to the door. I pulled it open, surprised to see Jaxson on the opposite side. "I wasn't expecting to see you today," I said.

He'd left yesterday in a huff after the few kisses we'd shared.

"You lied to me about who you are. Your actual name is Ariella Ryan."

His eyes narrowed, and his hands bunched in fists at his sides. He looked beyond pissed. The tips of his ears were red, and they matched his cheeks.

I took a step back as he entered my house. I kept space between us, even though I didn't sense I was in physical danger.

"That was my married name. I've taken my maiden name, and I am legally Ariella Cole. I never lied to you."

"The hell you didn't!" His voice thundered.

I shivered and jumped from the intensity of his rage. "I was acquitted. I didn't know what my ex-husband was involved in," I said.

Didn't he believe me? I wasn't a thief or a monster. I wasn't the one behind bars doing jail time for stealing millions.

"The hell you didn't! You owned a yacht, a mansion, and had a vacation home in the South Pacific!"

"I didn't know about those purchases," I said. It was the truth.

I didn't know about the additional bank account or luxuries that Benjamin had indulged in. While we were married, he had signed my name and forged it to further involve me in his illegal affairs.

He stalked closer, hovering within my personal space. "I don't believe you," he seethed.

"I'm telling the truth," I whispered, staring up at him and into his icy blue stare. "I knew the business had done well, but I didn't know where the money came from. I was naïve, and I trusted a man who took advantage of me." I took a step back, the heat radiating off his body and onto mine.

"Where's the money you stole?" He followed me, my back against the wall with nowhere to go.

"I didn't steal anything," I said and stood my ground. "I'm not a thief. My ex-husband was responsible, and he's in prison for what he did."

One hand came up against the wall, trapping me. His body was inches from mine. "I was one of your ex-husband's clients," Jaxson said, his breath hot against my cheek.

"I'm sorry," I said, quick to apologize. "I don't know what you want me to do." My voice was barely above a whisper, staring into his icy gaze.

It didn't take a genius to see he was angry, but it wasn't my fault. Didn't he realize that?

"The government froze all our accounts. They took the money that he'd stolen and redistributed it." At least that's what I thought happened.

His nostrils flared as he huffed. He was still pissed at me, but didn't he realize that's why I left? He wasn't too fond of me getting a fresh start. "Tell me why that's my problem."

I opened my mouth and quickly shut it. I had to tread carefully so as not to further antagonize him.

"It's not your problem. It's mine. I will get you the money for the refrigerator. I swear I will pay you back."

As soon as I landed a job, the first thing I would do was return him the money that he'd loaned me.

He pulled back, pacing the length of the cabin. "It's not about the money for the stupid refrigerator. It's the fact you lied to me, Ariella. Do you not see how that makes me look? I had to hear about it from Mason that you're a liar."

"I'm not a liar." I had neglected to give him information on my history, but we'd just met. Why would he think I'd have confided in him about my past?

I pushed myself away from the wall and folded my arms across my chest, coming to sit at the edge of the mattress.

"You're an asshole," I said, glaring at him.

"Excuse me?"

"You heard me." My hands trembled, but I shoved them farther into the arms of my shirt so that he wouldn't notice.

Anger raged through me. How dare he not believe me? Was he planning on interfering with me getting the job at Blue Sky Resort? That had to have been how he'd found out, through the background check.

Shit.

Was that reason enough for it to disqualify me for the position?

"All I did for you, and I'm the asshole." His jaw was tight, and he headed for the door. He pulled the door open and allowed a cold gust of wind to blow into the cabin.

I refrained from shivering, not wanting him to see my discomfort.

"Good luck at your new job and your new life," he shouted and slammed the door shut on his way out.

"Fuck!" I screamed and stood in the middle of the cabin, infuriated. I could see him outside, hurrying into his truck and speeding off down the road.

I couldn't keep running, no matter how hard it got.

———

I started my new job and orientation at Blue Sky Resort on Monday morning. While Jaxson knew about my past and my history, my employer hadn't been made aware.

I couldn't help but wonder if he had something to do with that or the fact my record had truly been expunged since I was exonerated.

I wasn't the only new employee, which was a relief. Emma and I spent the first month getting to know the routine and shared lunch every afternoon. It was nice to have someone to talk to, and who didn't know about my past.

"Do you want to grab drinks after work?" Emma asked. She worked behind the front desk while I had spent most of the first month handing out ski and snowboard equipment. It wasn't too bad, except for the occasional smelly boots that were returned and needed to be sprayed with disinfectant.

While I had little money, it was also payday, which meant I could afford to splurge on a drink. I needed to make friends and wanted to spend time some place other than my cabin or the resort.

"That would be fantastic," I said. "Do you know of any good bars around town?" It was already nearing the end of our workday, and I was antsy to get out.

"Well, it's not a bar, but they have great food and serve drinks. It's just up the road, Lumberjack Shack."

I groaned. Why did she have to suggest the one place Jaxson had taken me on my first night in

Breckenridge? Lincoln owned the place, and Jaxson was friends with him, which meant we could run into each other.

"Oh, is something wrong with that place?"

I hadn't realized she'd heard my sound of discontent. "No."

I didn't have a good excuse and wasn't ready to confide in her about my past or that I was formerly Ariella Ryan. She didn't need to know about my ex-husband or the crimes he had committed in both of our names. I also wasn't ready to talk about Jaxson with anyone yet.

"Okay, good." Emma's brow furrowed. "I don't know too many places in town. I'm still new here too."

Was it that obvious that I wasn't from Breckenridge or even Montana? "Where did you move from?" I asked. I hadn't realized she was new to town. At least we had something else in common other than our employer.

"I'm from California. Lived on the west coast my entire life, in Los Angeles."

"Tired of the city life?" I guessed. Why would anyone leave sunny weather to come here? Unless she had a secret of her own?

"I used to come out here with my family—my sister and her kids—for vacation."

Well, at least she was familiar with the area if she used to vacation in or around Breckenridge. "Did you come to the resort with your family?"

"We didn't stay at Blue Sky, but they snowboarded down the slopes while I took in some other sights." Emma winked at me. Her brown eyes glinted in the light before she glanced at her watch. "If you know the way to Lumberjack Shack, I'll meet you there."

"Sounds good." I grabbed my purse and headed to my car.

I was grateful Declan had managed a few minimal repairs and offered me a set of tire chains. He showed me how to put the chains on my tires and made it clear that I wasn't to drive with them on all the time, only when I drove on the snow covered terrain, specifically up the mountain.

I wouldn't get stuck again. Hopefully.

Declan had picked me up in his tow truck before work on my first day, early. I'd squared up with him on the payment and driven to the resort for orientation, making it just in time.

My credit card was nearly maxed, and since I didn't have full liability on the car, I wouldn't get a cent from insurance to help pay for the damages. Declan had been quiet on the drive to get my car, and I was grateful he hadn't mentioned Jaxson's name once.

Unlocking the door of my car, goose-pimples formed on my arms, and a chill ran down my spine. Someone watched me. I just knew it. I spun around, keys in hand to use as a weapon if I was in danger.

No one was behind me.

There were a few people in the parking lot. Still, I didn't recognize any of them: a family with their trunk open retrieving ski equipment, a woman buckling her young daughter into a car seat, and a gentleman wearing a baseball cap and a light jacket standing by his vehicle.

The guy alone, with the thin leather, seemed out of place. The baseball cap could have been a ruse, so I wouldn't recognize him. I tried not to stare.

My mind played tricks on me. I'd been concerned that someone would discover who I was, Ariella Ryan, and would come after me for the money my ex-husband stole. It had happened before when we lived in New York.

I climbed into my car and took off out of the parking lot and for the main road into town. The resort was about forty miles south of where I lived. The winter had been surprisingly mild and the snow that had fallen began to melt, making the road sludgy and wet. Declan had put a new set of tires on my car, and while they'd been previously used, they still had more life than my bald ones that hadn't given me anything but a headache.

There wasn't any music on the radio, the channels too far from where we lived. My car didn't have satellite radio, so I had to resort to popping in a CD for tunes. I traveled up the mountain, the slush recently plowed to the side, probably from one of the townspeople.

The sun began to set, but not before I pulled up in front of Lincoln's restaurant.

I didn't see any sign of Emma's car yet, but I'd left a little ahead of her. I glanced at my cell phone. She hadn't called, which at least was good news. She wasn't canceling on me.

I headed for the front entrance, the wooden door heavy as I swung it open. There wasn't a hostess, and no one took reservations even in season during the busiest months.

A sign by the front entrance read 'seat yourself,' so I grabbed a seat at the bar and put my coat down on the second stool to save Emma a seat.

The bartender's back was to me. His tight jeans and dark black t-shirt hung to his curves. I licked my dry lips and glanced him over. His butt looked pretty damned good.

I hadn't even had a man to fantasize about in ages. My ex-husband hadn't been dynamite in the sack. His needs had always come first, and then when he was done, so was I.

"Can I get a leg spreader?" I asked cheekily.

The bartender spun around and faced me.

The smile on my face fell to the floor. My stomach tensed. "Jaxson," I whispered and cleared my throat. His eyes locked on mine. "What are you doing here?"

I tried to sound confident in my question, like seeing him didn't tear apart my heart after the fight we'd had at my house.

"Don't you work at Eagle Tactical?" I asked. Had he changed careers recently? Did something happen between him and his military buddies? He'd been hostile toward me. Was there more to it I didn't know?

He grabbed a rag and wiped the wooden counter, his eyes avoiding me. "Just helping Lincoln out. Friday nights are always busy here, and I got off work early."

"Right." I glanced over my shoulder, hoping Emma would be here soon. I could use her support right now. I wasn't sure how much more I could take of Jaxson, talking with him, pretending like everything was okay, because it wasn't.

"I'll make you a special drink," he said and grabbed a shot glass from beneath the counter.

I wordlessly watched as he sliced a jalapeno pepper in half and placed it into the shot glass.

My stomach somersaulted. I wasn't keen on spicy drinks or foods. Then he poured tequila and several dashes of hot sauce into the glass before sliding the concoction across the bar.

"Your Anus Burner. Enjoy." His eyes twinkled with mirth before he headed across the bar to help another patron.

"I guess I deserved that," I muttered under my breath.

"What's that?" Emma asked.

I spun around on my chair and removed my coat. "I saved you a seat."

"I saw you met the bartender." She sat down and leaned against the bar, waving at Jaxson to get his attention. "Jaxson!"

He ignored Emma because she was with me. "My apologies in advance if he makes you a shitty drink. We're not on the best-speaking terms."

"Wait, you know my boyfriend?" Emma shifted to face me.

My eyes widened, and I sipped the drink so that I didn't have to say anything, momentarily forgetting about the hot and disgusting concoction until it touched my lips.

I coughed and tried not to gag.

"We're neighbors," I said, not wanting to confide anything else. How long had they been together? Jaxson hadn't mentioned it when we'd first met, but that had been over a month ago.

CHAPTER FOURTEEN

JAXSON

What the hell was she doing at the bar? It wasn't bad enough that Ariella had shown up for drinks, but now Emma joined her.

Were they seriously friends?

I wanted to go outside and shoot something.

"Jaxson!" Emma's voice echoed across the bar, but I ignored her. Was there any chance she'd just go away?

I could see her waving to me, leaning across the bar, trying to get my attention.

I exhaled a heavy breath. I couldn't ignore her forever, even if I wanted to.

It wasn't bad enough dealing with Ariella, but now I had to face the mother of my child, the woman who had stomped on my heart and given up Izzie. I'd already confronted her and hoped that she'd have gone back to California, but it seemed I wasn't that lucky.

Swallowing the bile rising in my throat, I put on a fake smile, all cheer.

"Isn't he great?" Emma said with a thousand-watt grin. She was putting on all the charm. Two could play at that game.

"Yeah," Ariella said. She nursed her shot glass but had barely touched it. She shifted on the stool, looking mighty uncomfortable.

Was it from the Anus Burner or the fact she wasn't expecting to see me? I wasn't too pleased to run into her, either.

"What do you want, Emma?"

Emma batted her eyelashes, smiling up at me with a smug grin. "Aside from you?"

"That's not part of the menu," I said, trying to keep it professional.

Did Ariella know Emma was Isabella's mother? They'd both been hired by Blue Sky Resort.

Were they now friends? I didn't want to ask because I wasn't prepared for the answer.

Ariella sipped her drink and grimaced.

"You're going to swallow it all down, every last drop," I said, staring at Ariella.

God, I was turned on right now, watching her fingers stroke the rim of the shot glass.

How long had it been since I'd been with a woman? The fact I couldn't remember meant it was too damned long.

She lifted the glass to her lips, mouth parted, and drank the disgusting concoction that I'd had the displeasure of trying many years ago, thanks to my military buddies.

Ariella's eyes slammed shut and winced as she swallowed the drink, slamming the empty shot glass against the wooden bar top. "I want a Screwdriver," Ariella said, matter of factly.

Emma glanced from Ariella to me, her brow furrowed. "Make me a Sex on the Beach."

"You'll get what I give you," I said. We weren't done by any stretch.

I grabbed a shaker and mixed ice, vodka, orange juice, lemon juice, and triple sec. Then I strained it over ice and topped it with ginger ale.

I handed the drink to Emma.

"Well, at least it's not what you had," Emma said to Ariella.

"Enjoy your Golden Shower." I grabbed another glass from beneath the bar to make Ariella a drink.

Emma stared at the liquor, a look of disgust on her face. "Why do you have to be such an ass?"

"That's what I said," Ariella chimed in. "Well, I don't remember if I said it aloud, but I thought it," she muttered.

"Don't worry, your drink is next," I said. "I didn't forget you." As much as I despised Emma, Ariella frustrated me, but I didn't hate her.

Not really.

I'd had a month to sit on the news that she'd lied and didn't tell me who she was. It had hurt, but we weren't together. She didn't owe me anything.

I didn't want to point out that I'd been harsh, and I sure as shit would not apologize, but I had to do something.

"I'm not sure I'm thirsty," Ariella said, glancing at Emma's drink.

I grabbed another shaker and mixed it with ice, vodka, peach schnapps, orange juice, and cranberry juice. I'd had this concoction and had rather enjoyed it, even with its name.

I served her drink over ice, sliding the glass to Ariella. "Enjoy your Tight Snatch," I said, staring at her, refusing to back down.

"Why couldn't you have made me that?" Emma said, reaching for Ariella's drink.

Ariella whisked it out of Emma's reach and brought the glass to her lips, a faint smile on her face. "You know just what I like."

Was she trying to flirt with me?

I'd been an ass to her tonight and was she trying to reconnect with me? Was it the alcohol talking?

I'd cut her off with the second drink. I didn't need her getting into an accident on her way home tonight.

"Hey, ladies," Declan said, coming over to the bar. He put one arm around Ariella and the other around Emma.

"Declan!" Emma squealed, her eyes widening. "Can you please tell this grump to make me a drink that I'd like?"

Declan snorted and pointed at the yellow-tinged drink. "What'd he make you?" he asked.

"A Golden Shower," I said and grinned. "We all know she deserves it."

"Ouch," Declan said and stepped away from the ladies.

He came around to the other side, going behind the bar. He turned to face me, keeping his voice low so that only I could hear him. "Take the night off. You're not doing Lincoln any favors antagonizing the customers."

I wasn't one to walk away or back down. "Lincoln asked for my help."

"Yeah, but I don't think he's going to appreciate when his customers don't come back because you're giving them disgusting drinks."

"My Tight Snatch is pretty good," Ariella said. They could hear our private conversation. She sipped her drink, offering me a warm smile.

Declan grabbed me by the arm and dragged me around to the back room, out of earshot of any customers. "What the hell is going on?"

"Emma is now friends with Ariella!" I couldn't just let it go.

It wasn't bad enough Emma had returned, but now she was making friends around town. To me, that meant she wasn't planning on leaving soon.

"Oh, the horror," Declan said with a laugh and rolled his eyes. "I've seen you face down, far worse and not break a sweat. These two women have you in a tizzy, Jaxson. Go home, clear your head."

"I can't do that." I wouldn't leave. Lincoln needed me, and I hadn't seen Ariella in a month.

As angry as I was with her, I was glad to see her. It meant she was still in Breckenridge and hadn't left because of me.

"Shit, man. You're smitten. I'm just not sure for which one."

I folded my arms across my chest, my face neutral. "You're confused."

"I think you're the one who is confused," Declan said. "I know you're upset with Emma, but she told you about Izzie. You could give her a second chance."

Emma?

Did he think I had feelings for Emma still? "Emma's the mother of my child, but that's it. I can't even look at her in that way, knowing she wanted to give up Izzie, my daughter, to a stranger."

"Well, she did the right thing. She didn't lie about not knowing who the father was, and she came to you. That couldn't have been easy."

He was right. It wasn't easy for either of them. "This isn't about Emma."

"Of course, it's not." Declan's eyes narrowed. "So, it's about Ariella?"

"No," I said, answering a little too quickly and forcefully.

Declan grinned. "Okay, good. I know she's got a past, but she's hot. If you're not going to ask her out or pursue her, I will."

"Don't you dare!" The thought of Declan taking Ariella home boiled my blood.

Smirking, he walked backward out of the hall and approached the bar. "Never took you for the jealous type."

"Fuck," I muttered under my breath as I headed back out to help bartend. "Me either."

At first glance, I didn't see Ariella or Emma. They'd both gotten up and were now dancing to the music that had been cranked up louder.

Drink in hand, Ariella swayed to the music. Her hips were doing things that made my body respond in ways I wasn't prepared for tonight.

I found it difficult to focus on anything but her as I stood behind the bar.

Ariella locked eyes with me and smiled. Whether it was the drinks or the fact she was having fun, I couldn't tell.

She nodded in my direction, acknowledging me.

I tore my gaze away from her. She'd lied to me, fooled me into believing she needed help and money, and I'd been the sucker to buy her a damned refrigerator.

I hated myself for it, but even more so, I hated Ariella for how she made me feel.

A gentleman I didn't recognize sauntered over to her, dancing up against her, coming between Ariella and Emma.

The younger man was shorter than I am and a few pounds heavier, but not in muscle.

I didn't have to worry about him stealing her interest, right? He wasn't that attractive.

Ariella laughed and feigned a smile.

Was she talking to him? I couldn't believe he'd earned her time. I stared down at the counter, grabbed a rag, scrubbed at the wood, and rubbed at it hard as if that would take away the anger and pain that radiated through my chest.

I refused to lift my gaze upward.

I didn't want to witness another man flirting with Ariella. Even if I was pissed at her, she was off-limits to anyone else.

My hands bunched into fists, and I threw the rag on the floor. My feet slammed against the tile as I came around from behind the bar.

Her blue eyes widened on my approach, and she shifted awkwardly, holding up a hand to tell the gentleman to back off. "Please back off," Ariella said.

Her voice was soft, tentative, not the least bit threatening.

"Come on, now," the man groaned and stepped closer. His lips hovered by her ear as he whispered something to her.

I hurried across the dance floor, wanting to make sure she was all right.

I stepped between him and Ariella and threw my arm around her. "Sorry I'm late, babe," I said and planted my lips on hers.

I was saving her ass or about to get sucker punched.

CHAPTER FIFTEEN

ARIELLA

Out of nowhere, he kissed me.

I opened my mouth to ask Jaxson what the hell he was doing when his tongue glided into my mouth, which only made me further speechless.

Sweat trickled down my forehead, and my heart raced as I stopped moving on the dance floor.

My body responded to his tongue in my mouth and his hands around my hips, pulling me closer, tighter, harder. He was nestled up against my thigh.

I swallowed the lump in my throat and slowly pulled back.

Jaxson stared at me. His fingers moved over my lower back and slid beneath my shirt.

I shivered from his touch.

My insides melted and made my knees tremble.

"Looks like he's gone," Jaxson said, though his eyes never seemed to leave my gaze.

"What? Oh, right." Was that why he had kissed me intimately, to ward off the drunk loser who wouldn't take no for an answer?

I'd been handling it.

Then he swooped in and locked lips with me. I leaned closer, and my breath caressed his ear with a whisper. "I guess I should thank you for coming to my rescue."

Emma hadn't been the least bit helpful. She was nowhere in sight, and I'd just been dancing with her a moment earlier. "Where'd Emma go?" I untangled from Jaxson's embrace.

"She probably left when I started kissing you."

"Emma likes you," I said.

I didn't want to come between them if they were involved.

His hands didn't untangle from mine, his fingers caressing my lower back against my bare skin in soothing motions. His touch had a way of being hypnotic, lulling me closer to him.

"What Emma and I had ended long before you got here," Jaxson said.

Did Emma know that?

She'd called him her boyfriend when they'd first gotten to the bar. Did she just want it to be true?

"I work with Emma. She's one of the few friends I've made in town." She was the only friend I had anywhere.

I had alienated everyone back home, and I didn't want to do that here.

This was my second chance, a fresh start where almost no one knew my past.

"Did she tell you she's Izzie's birth mother?" Jaxson asked.

"What?" I took a step back, the news hitting me like a knife to my chest. The bar was steamy, suffocating.

I slipped from Jaxson's embrace and down the hall, needing to find the door outside.

I needed air.

I needed to cool off before I got sick from the news.

Stumbling through the throes of customers, I found my way down the hallway and out a back exit, into the frosty night air.

Darkness enveloped the sky. The new moon offered no light, and while stars had been abundant, it didn't help me see so much as my hands in front of me.

I leaned forward, taking several deep breaths. I didn't need to see to know that I was on the verge of throwing up.

It probably had more to do with the adrenaline spiking through my system than anything else, but I was worn and exhausted.

"Ariella," Jaxson said, hurrying outside after me. He rested a warm and reassuring hand on my back.

I wanted to pull away from him, to tell him not to touch me, that I didn't belong with him, but I couldn't do it.

The words didn't come.

My body was too tired to speak, too exhausted to explain my racing thoughts. I could never make him happy, not in the way Emma could.

"Just breathe," he said, rubbing my back over my sweater.

It was frigid outside without a coat, and only now had I felt anything but the heat of an inferno raging inside of me.

"You're shivering. Do you think you can make it back inside? I can find us a quiet place to sit down."

Nodding, I didn't speak. I forgot that he probably couldn't see much in the darkness. "Yes," I said.

He led me back into the bar, through the crowd of guests, both locals and out-of-towners vacationing and staying at the resort. Jaxson took my hand and wordlessly led me up the back staircase.

"Where are we going?" I finally asked, fatigued from the adrenaline rush earlier.

Some people found the fight-or-flight reflex stimulating. I found it exhausting.

I never understood people who liked bungee jumping or throwing themselves out of an airplane with a parachute. I preferred a far less exciting lifestyle.

"Lincoln has a place upstairs. We can crash there for a little while. It beats outside, and when you're feeling better, I can drive you home."

He probably thought I couldn't hold my liquor, and while I was a lightweight, one had nothing to do with the other.

Jaxson unlocked the door, flipped on the light, and led me inside, a hand on my lower back as he guided me to sit down on the sofa. "Thank you," I whispered, staring up at him.

He seemed to be on a mission, opening the fridge, helping himself to something. Apparently, Lincoln wouldn't mind.

"Drink this," he said, bringing me a bottle of water. "Do you need crackers too?" He handed me the water and then, before I could answer, started tearing apart the cabinets searching, presumably, for crackers.

"This will be fine. Thank you." My hands trembled as I sat on the couch. I struggled to open the stupid bottle of water.

Most people never noticed the tremor, but when my adrenaline beat me at my game of trying to be tough, it became pretty obvious.

"How many drinks did you have tonight? Did that jerk come anywhere near your drink?" Jaxson frowned. His brow furrowed as he came to sit beside me on the sofa. "Shit."

"What?" I asked. Had he just now noticed the tremor? "No, I didn't let anyone but you near my drinks tonight. I only had two. It's not that big of a deal."

I shoved the plastic water bottle and my hands between my legs, hoping to stop the shaking, but it wasn't just my hands trembling. My legs were bouncing too.

Fuck, I hated my body. It betrayed me whenever I had a surge of emotions that made my heart race.

Sitting down had helped immensely, and while the tremors hadn't settled, I no longer had the pit of my stomach heavy like I was going to throw up or pass out.

He took notice of the bottle unopened in my grasp and took it from me, loosening the lid before he handed it back. "Is this my fault?"

Why was he jumping to that conclusion?

How could it possibly be his fault? "Jaxson, you're not making any sense." I sipped the water, using two hands to keep from spilling the contents all over me. The damned tremor wasn't helping me, either.

Why couldn't I live a normal life like everyone else?

Why did I have to be unfortunate enough to be in my mid-thirties with an autonomic nervous system that hated me? I had dealt with it on my own for years, but it freaked out new people.

"The drink I made for you," he said, staring at my hands, watching as I brought the water bottle to my lips for another sip. "I was an asshole."

"You were mad," I said, having forgiven him. He'd rescued me on the dance floor. That searing, passionate kiss also helped. I'd be thinking about it for the next month. "I can assure you the disgusting drink you made didn't do this."

"Do I need to call a doctor? Your face is flushed."

"My heart is racing too," I said and laughed. I was used to the symptoms, and I just hated when they took over my life. "Relax. Just sit with me." I liked his company, though I wasn't sure I was ready to confess that much to him yet.

"Okay," he said and sat back on the sofa. He didn't look the least bit relaxed. Jaxson shifted one leg over the other. Then put his foot down, rearranging his position on the sofa before putting two feet down.

I sat there, not moving, watching him literally squirm in his seat. "Do you have ants in your pants?"

"I'm glad you're feeling up to making a joke and finding all of this funny."

"I wouldn't go that far," I said, bringing the water bottle to my lips for another swig. "I guess I'm just used to this, and while it's not fun, I usually can sense the spiral before the downfall."

"Does this happen a lot?" Jaxson asked. He leaned forward, his hands folded together in his lap, his eyes never leaving mine.

I wasn't used to talking about my health issues with anyone other than my physician back home. I needed to find a new doctor in Breckenridge, though a neurologist who specialized in autonomic disorders would not be easy to come by.

"It happens from time to time." I didn't elaborate. I wasn't sure I wanted to confide in him. Everyone I trusted always betrayed me.

"We don't have to talk about it if it's making you uncomfortable," Jaxson said.

Exhaling a loud sigh, I leaned back on the couch, letting the leather sofa cradle my body as much as possible. It was far more comfortable than my sofa at home. Eventually, I'd want to get new furniture, but I had bills to pay. "Where's Izzie?" I asked.

"She's at home with my sister, who is in town for the week."

"Why aren't you home with your family?" That surprised me, though. I didn't know that much about him. We hadn't been on speaking terms until today.

Jaxson stretched out, his arm falling around my shoulders on the back of the couch.

I glanced at him, and he shot me a coy smile before refocusing his attention on the wall. "She's a handful."

"Your sister or Izzie?"

"Both." Jaxson snorted with a laugh under his breath. "Izzie has been testing my patience like all three-year-olds do, and my sister, Skylar, is just about as annoying as Izzie."

I held my tongue, smiling as I stared at Jaxson. "Does she live far away?" I asked.

"She's about a four-hour drive, which means she's not planning on leaving tonight."

"That's too bad. I was hoping you'd show me your bedroom, but I guess if you have a houseguest," I said, teasing him.

He groaned. "You're killing me."

"Somehow, I doubt that," I said, shifting to face him. I rested my hand on his chest and patted his shirt reassuringly. "I think you can handle a little family time. You're a tough guy. I mean, you do that Eagle Tactical stuff for a living."

I didn't know all that it entailed, but it was a high-adrenaline job, something I could never do.

While I had previously held a high-profile job, my responsibilities had never held the same type of risk. I'd been assigned surveillance from a computer, often behind a desk in an office somewhere around the globe. Another secret.

He grabbed my wrist, his fingers interlocking with mine. "Are you always a tease?" Jaxson asked and leaned closer.

One hand held mine. The other that had snaked around the sofa was now tangled in my hair. He pulled me closer and onto his lap.

Startled, I spilled the open bottle of water all over his shirt and pants.

He shrieked from the cold, and I leaped off his body like I'd just mutilated him.

My hand rested over my heart, realizing what happened. "You're going to give me a heart attack."

"Well, at least you don't look like you came in your pants."

I snickered under my breath. While I tried not to grin, it seemed an impossible task. "You could have peed yourself?"

"Right, because that is so much better."

"Snarky is not your color," I said.

He grabbed a hand towel from the kitchen and patted down his pants to dry them off in a lame attempt.

"Do you need a hand?" I sat on the sofa, watching him, waiting for him to settle down.

He kept blotting at his soaking wet crotch, his shirt damp forgotten.

That didn't seem to bother him.

"No one's going to see. It's just you and me up here."
I reminded him we were alone. "There's probably a
dryer around here. You can take off your clothes and
shove them in the dryer. Turn it on for a few
minutes."

"You would like that, wouldn't you? Was that your
plan all along?" He removed his shirt first, balling it
up and throwing it at me on the sofa.

His hands went to the button on his jeans,
unclasping it before sliding the zipper down.

Time stood still as I held my breath, waiting for him
to finish undressing.

"Yes, you caught me. I wanted to get you naked in
Lincoln's house," I said and covered my enormous
smile that seemed impossible to hide.

Jaxson slid his jeans down and tossed the denim
at me.

"Are you expecting me to do your laundry? In case
you haven't realized, this isn't the 1950s." I couldn't
take my eyes off of him.

Shirtless, he had an impressive body. He didn't need
a tan to show off his muscles.

My eyes fell over his body, examining every inch that I could see, his boxers getting in the way of anything more exciting.

"Lucky for you," Jaxson said. He stalked toward me, leaning forward, half-naked.

I exhaled a heavy breath.

My body responded in kind, wanting to touch him, taste him, and explore everything he had to offer. I struggled to keep my eyes open, his body hovering, teasing me.

I shifted closer as he leaned in, wanting a kiss, a taste of what he offered. One kiss hadn't been enough earlier in the bar.

I craved more.

Being around him, half-naked, was stirring my insides and making me restless beneath him. He hovered above me, his eyes boring into mine.

Jaxson snatched his wet clothes from my grasp, leaving me breathless and panting.

"Such a tease," I muttered under my breath.

A voice by the door cleared his throat, albeit rather loudly, to get our attention.

Jaxson took a step back, wet clothes in hand, as he spun around to see who had come inside the apartment.

"You two couldn't make it back to Jaxson's place?" Lincoln asked. He shut the door behind himself and stalked into the kitchen, his footsteps heavy against the floor.

It wasn't a rhetorical question.

"Please do me a favor and don't do anything on that sofa. I like it and would hate to have to throw it out or burn it after Jaxson's ass gets all over the leather."

Lincoln had a sense of humor. I laughed and covered my lips. "We were just coming up here to rest." It was a lame excuse, but I didn't want to tell him the real reason and face his pity.

"Of course, you were." He glanced at Jaxson as he stood in nothing but his boxers and a smile.

"Believe it or not, she spilled water on me, and I was just about to put my clothes in your dryer," Jaxson said.

"That's a new excuse, and I don't buy it," Lincoln said.

Jaxson stared at me, waiting for my input. "Give me a hand here."

I took another sip of the near-empty water bottle. "You're doing just fine."

It was fun to see him flustered and being teased by his friend.

Lincoln didn't appear mad, and while he probably wasn't thrilled to walk in on guests in his home, he wasn't kicking us out yet, either.

Lincoln pointed at Jaxson. "Is this guy trying to take advantage of you, because if he is, I'll kick his ass?" He approached Jaxson, holding out his hand for the wet clothes.

Was he checking to see if I'd spilled water on him?

"He's quite the gentleman," I said.

Lincoln grunted under his breath, satisfied with the wet clothes. "I'll throw this into the dryer. You can borrow something of mine from the dresser. I'd rather not have you half-naked in my living room."

"Aw," I whined in protest. "I was enjoying the show."

Lincoln thudded with heavy footsteps down the hall, wet clothes in hand. "Well, I wasn't, and I live here."

"Fair enough." I finished the last of my water, already feeling much better. Perhaps it was the banter, the fact both men had taken my mind off everything else that had been bothering me.

I hadn't realized Jaxson had disappeared down the hall until he returned to the living room wearing a pair of gray sweats and a black t-shirt.

"Now, where were we?" Jaxson asked, approaching the sofa. He stood in front of me, hovered above as I stared up at him. His legs straddled mine, teasing me without so much as touching me.

I whimpered in protest. Being in his proximity, having seen him half-undressed moments earlier, had made me crave him even more.

As if the kiss hadn't been my initial undoing.

"You were just about to tell me why you don't have a girlfriend," I said.

CHAPTER SIXTEEN

JAXSON

"I can answer that," Lincoln interrupted as he stomped back into the living room.

"I'd rather you didn't," I shot out, hoping he would mind his own business.

I glared at Lincoln, warning him to shut the hell up.

He had no trouble finding dates with the ladies. He'd always been able to pick up any girl he wanted in a bar and bring her home. It didn't hurt that the restaurant he worked and owned had a bar and a bedroom upstairs.

I didn't want to think about all the women he'd had on the couch where Ariella sat.

She stared up at me with dark, soulful eyes, her cheeks still red but not as flushed as she'd been earlier when I brought her upstairs to rest. "Don't you have meals to make and guests to tend to?" I asked.

"I came upstairs to find out why you weren't manning the bar. Imagine my surprise when I found you and Ariella up in my place, already undressed."

"It really was because I spilled water on him," Ariella said, her voice soft and timid. Was she afraid of Lincoln? He was a big guy, same as I was, same as the rest of our band of brothers who served.

"Just don't leave a stain on the couch. I don't want to have to replace that sofa," he quipped before retreating out the door and back down the stairs.

"I hope I didn't get you into any trouble," Ariella said as her eyes fell toward her lap.

I reached down, my thumb guiding her chin up to face me. I wanted to stare into her eyes, see the truth, know what she was thinking.

It was dangerous, investing my time and energy into a woman who might never want to commit. That was the easy part.

She'd lied to me, and I still couldn't let that go, the nagging suspicion that there might still have been more she wasn't telling me.

My body had betrayed me, kissing her on the dance floor, and while I usually kept a level head, I couldn't seem to do that around her.

I released my grip on her chin, unable to tear my gaze away from her, transfixed.

"You never answered my question," Ariella whispered, staring up at me.

I let out a heavy sigh, unsure how to answer. It was far more complicated than just not having a girlfriend. She knew about Izzie. "Isabella is a lifelong commitment. Let's just say not everyone feels the same way."

"I don't believe that," Ariella whispered. She reached for my hand and nodded beside her at the empty seat on the sofa.

I collapsed onto the leather, the material sinking around my body comfortable after a long day. "I don't want to waste my time with a woman who isn't interested in being around for the long run."

"What about Emma?" she asked. "Why aren't you with her?"

I ran a hand through my hair, ruffling it. She sure knew how to ask the hard questions. "I don't love her."

Could the answer be as simple as that?

It was the truth.

We hadn't ever been in love.

"Oh," Ariella said, her voice soft as her mouth formed a little "o" shape.

"She came to town a few years ago for a family vacation with her sister and her kids. While they went snowboarding, she came to the bar for drinks. That's how we met. We both got trashed and ended up at my place."

It was literally as simple as it sounded. I left out the part where I had gotten hammered after my sister had come for a visit and just left. The house was quiet, empty, and I needed to dull my heart from her nagging and blaming me for our father's death.

"Well, it's obvious to me that she wants you back." She shifted on the sofa, pulling slightly away, dragging her legs up onto the leather and to the side, tucking them under herself.

I'd seen how Emma had acted today, and I couldn't say I was surprised.

I'd been shocked when I discovered she had moved to Breckenridge for a job.

After the initial anger, the disgust had worn off. She had a right to live wherever she wanted, but that didn't mean I had to give her custody or let her see Isabella. That wasn't a conversation I needed to have with Ariella.

"Wanting someone back implies they were theirs to have originally. That was never the case. We were never friends or lovers. We had one drunken afternoon together, and it had been a poor lapse in judgment." It had been the only time I'd engaged in a one-night stand and look where it got me.

"She didn't tell me that."

I wouldn't have expected her to. While I didn't know Emma incredibly well, I also didn't think she would be forthright with information, even if she and Ariella were friends.

"I'm not surprised. It didn't work to her advantage. She thinks we're more than we are, especially after Izzie."

I didn't want Emma.

I wasn't sure I even wanted to risk my heart with Ariella, but I would regret not trying. There was something about her that captivated me.

"What about you? Any more secrets that I should know about?" I asked.

She pursed her lips, her eyes tightening. "I'm literally an open book on the internet. Search my name, and you can find every detail of my life."

Was it that simple? "Is that why you didn't tell me your real name?" I asked.

Was she worried I couldn't handle knowing who she was? It hadn't been my best day, learning that her ex-husband had been responsible for stealing investors' money.

I no longer blamed her for any involvement. She'd been prosecuted and acquitted. While I hadn't followed her case as closely as I'd followed her ex-husband's, I had done a little research after I'd discovered that she'd lied to me.

"I wanted a second chance to start over. There had been threats made against my life when I was married to that scum-sucking bastard. Bricks were thrown through our windows, and someone sprayed graffiti on the siding and doors. For months, I had been afraid to go home, sleeping in my car where I worked. That didn't last. I got fired, and while I had been acquitted, it wasn't like they were offering me my job back. They told me I was bad publicity and too much of a risk."

I could sense her frustration.

Her tone had grown louder, more determined as she spoke. She sat up straighter and pushed a strand of her dark hair behind her ear.

"I thought no publicity was bad publicity," I said. I guess that wasn't true.

"That's a lie," Ariella said.

I tried to keep a level head, remain calm.

Hearing her life had been in danger worried me. I'd dealt with some unhinged people in my line of work. "Have the threats stopped since moving here?" I asked. She'd tell me if she was in danger, wouldn't she?

Slowly, she nodded. "No one seems to know who I am. As long as that continues, I should be fine. I just keep hoping that with time it'll all blow over." She twirled the edge of her long dark hair. "I'm not sure if you know this, but I was blonde when it all happened—the trial, the threats, the news media. Having long dark hair has made it so no one recognizes me."

I liked her hair.

Hell, I liked almost everything about her.

I wasn't too happy about her past, but I accepted it. Letting out a soft breath, my fingers tangling in her curls.

I leaned forward. I wanted to kiss her, to take away her pain and the difficulty of her past. "I like your dark hair. I think it looks sexy," I whispered.

Everything about her was sexy, from her pouty bottom lip to the bounce in her step.

Her eyes slowly closed, and she leaned forward, our lips colliding as I pulled her closer. As I brought her onto my lap, the kiss deepened.

She shifted against my hips, making my insides roar to life with the sweet sounds she made of a soft moan from the back of her throat.

I wanted to devour her and taste every inch of her body, but we couldn't do it here, not in Lincoln's place above the bar.

I pulled back with all the strength I had, and my forehead pressed against hers. Listening to the soft, heavy gasps for air as she caught her breath, I stole one more kiss. "I should get you home and to bed," I whispered.

"I'd like that very much."

———

I led Ariella downstairs and quickly dropped off her car key with Lincoln.

He agreed to drive her car and drop it off later with Declan following and giving him a ride back home.

We scooted out the side door for privacy.

I kept her close, with one hand at her lower back, keeping her at my side in the darkness. I'd always had decent night vision, adjusting quicker than most.

I opened the passenger side door and helped her into the truck. I waited for her to buckle before I shut the door and came around to my side.

I wanted to follow her inside, take her home and ravish every ounce of her skin.

Would she invite me inside? I didn't want to be forceful or take advantage of the situation.

She had two drinks, but that had been quite a while ago. While she could have probably driven herself home, I didn't want to lose the opportunity to take care of her.

The ride was short and quick. I pulled up out front and hustled to the passenger door. Leading her to the dark cabin, I wanted to make sure she got inside safely, especially without a porch light.

"You should install solar lights outside," I said. I doubted she'd do much until the spring thaw. It was too cold to dig up the yard.

"I'll add that to my to-do list," Ariella said. She stood outside, keys in hand, fidgeting with them but not making any attempt to unlock the door.

I had no intention of leaving until she went inside. I shoved my hands into my coat pocket to keep warm and shuffled my feet. "I hope you're feeling better."

"I am. Thank you for that tonight. Do you want to come in? I can offer you coffee, a drink, or something else?" She chewed her bottom lip.

Ariella looked nervous.

I couldn't tell if she was hesitant or just worried I'd turn her down.

"I'd love that something else," I said, teasing her.

Her cheeks reddened, and I waited for her to unlock the door before I followed her inside. After a minute, she turned on the lantern and lit a few candles. It made for a nice, ambient glow.

"Can I get you something to drink?" Ariella offered. She removed her coat and boots. I did the same, keeping mine by the door.

"I'll have whatever you're having," I said as I approached the wood-burning stove.

I bent down and grabbed the handle to open the door. The hinge squeaked in protest. I made a mental note to fix that the next time I came over.

"I'm going to throw some wood on the fire." While I looked forward to climbing under the covers with Ariella, I also didn't want the cabin to be frigid.

However, it would give me an excuse to cuddle up against her and make her hot and sweaty.

Stoking the fire, bringing it roaring back to life, I tossed in a piece of wood and then another. Her gaze never left me. "See something you like?"

"Actually, yes," she said and sauntered over toward me.

With two bottles of beer in hand, she put them down on the coffee table and tugged on her bottom lip, pulling it between her teeth.

Was it a nervous habit or something else? I hadn't been around her enough to take note.

"What's that?" I asked, cocking a grin at her.

She gestured at my clothes. "You have too much on. I liked what I saw earlier tonight. Too bad Lincoln walked in."

"It was too bad, wasn't it?" I'd have to get my clothes tomorrow and return Lincoln's sweats.

I stalked toward her and pulled her into my arms, her body nestled tight against mine, a perfect fit. "Seems only fair, though, to see you in nothing but your underwear."

CHAPTER SEVENTEEN

ARIELLA

I swallowed the lump that formed in my throat.

Did he want to see me in my underwear?

Of course, he did, I had invited him into my house. I didn't think he only wanted a drink, did I?

"You first," I said, my lips almost touching his.

His body pressed tight against mine, his fingers caressed my lower back, just as he had earlier, inching my shirt up. His warm hands stroked my bare skin, but he didn't remove my shirt, just teased me.

Jaxson took a half step back, pulling his shirt up and over his head, letting it hit the floor with a thud. "Your turn."

Goosebumps from the chill in the air pebbled my arms, but my breathing came out louder, ragged, and heavy as warmth flooded my senses.

The room temperature hadn't changed. It was me, and I was the one getting hot and bothered by looking at Jaxson shirtless.

Could I let this happen?

There was still one more secret, a big one that he didn't know. I should have told him earlier tonight, when he asked, but I'd held onto that last piece and guarded it along with my heart.

When I didn't budge from my position, his fingers grazing my skin slid my shirt up, inch by inch, taking his time—lifting my arms into the air, letting him undress me if that's what he wanted to do.

He fell to his knees, his lips on my stomach, his breath warm and inviting, making my body unsteady.

"I need to tell you something."

His hands held my hips, keeping me against him as he kissed a warm path up my stomach and across my bra. Jaxson's fingers grazed over my breast, teasing me, tasting me with soft kisses as he pulled my shirt up and over my head, discarding it to the floor.

"Is it about your health?" he asked, pausing briefly, his gaze latched on mine.

I shook my head. "The doctor gives all clear," I said, forcing a smile along with my joke.

Sex, I could do. There were no rules against engaging in intimate physical activity.

While I wanted to tell him the truth about what I did for a living before I was fired, now didn't feel the right time.

"Then that's all that matters." He grinned, his eyes dark with want. He captured my lips in a searing, heated kiss, his fingers tangling in my hair, pulling me closer and tighter against his body.

"You still have too many clothes on. You weren't wearing sweats earlier," I reminded him as my hands went to his hips, caressing the waistband of the soft, stretchy material.

"Go ahead," he told me, giving me permission to undress him.

I hooked my fingers in both his sweats and his boxers, bringing it all down in one motion, bending down to guide his pants off. My eyes raked over his naked body, every inch of him.

I wanted to take him in my mouth, taste him, touch him, caress him in every way I knew how.

How long had it been since a woman dropped to her knees for him?

He cleared his throat, and that seemed to gather my attention as my gaze stared up at him.

"You're killing me," he groaned between gritted teeth. Jaxson hoisted me from the floor and planted my feet firmly on the ground, not allowing me to be on my knees.

I giggled unceremoniously, licking my bottom lip, wanting to taste him.

Jaxson lunged forward. His tongue swiped against my lips, and pushed into my mouth in haste.

With one hand on my hip, the other in my hair, he pulled me harder against him.

I still had my pants and bra on, and he stood naked. It seemed like a dream come true for me. I'd imagined what he looked like, what his skin was like under my touch, but I never thought I'd experience a night with him.

He pulled back, each breath heavy, his eyes narrowed. "Every time you stick that tongue out or chew that bottom lip, I'm going to kiss you, hard."

"Is that a threat?" I liked what he had in mind.

"Only you would take that as a challenge, Freckles," Jaxson growled out as he spoke.

I didn't want to admit how he drove me wild and my body flushed at the nickname he'd given me.

My insides were warm, and my heart pounded against my ribcage like a prisoner trying to break free. Heat burned over my skin and inside, waiting for sweet release.

My tongue darted out and dared him to kiss me hard. I wanted to experience what he had to offer. I liked this dance, the way we played, the not soft and sweet.

He grabbed my hips, yanked me toward him, and his mouth descended hard on mine. His tongue stroked my lips and pushed its way into my mouth.

I opened my lips and granted him access, allowing him whatever he wanted. I was at his mercy, willing to do anything and everything.

All he had to do was to take command.

He lifted me into his arms, and I wrapped my legs around his body. Jaxson carried me to the bed, our lips fused in passionate kisses, neither of us untangling first.

In haste, we hurried to the mattress, Jaxson's body covering mine, crawling above me, releasing my grip on his hips. I kept my mouth with his, fire fueled kisses never seeming to cease.

His hands pushed at my pants, and I offered help, lifting my hips so he could slide the material off. I moaned in protest when he pulled back from my lips. Sliding my slacks down my hips and kissing a trail between my thighs, he continued teasing me.

I grew restless, desiring more. "Please," I panted, already quite breathless. I lay on my back at his mercy, allowing him to do with me as he pleased.

"Please, what?" Jaxson asked, raising an eyebrow at me.

I wasn't sure what he wanted to hear. I wasn't above begging, but I was already doing that when his fingers teased against my panties, and he bent down, blowing softly over my center.

My insides throbbed to be touched, pleased, and satisfied. Was he going to tease me to oblivion? "Please, Sir?"

"Not what I was looking for, but I do like the sound of that," Jaxson crooned. "I never would have taken you for a submissive."

"I'm not," I countered defensively.

"There's nothing wrong if you are, Freckles," Jaxson said with a grin. His fingers grazed my heated core through my panties, but he hadn't removed my last two shreds of clothes yet, my panties or bra.

Growing restless, I shifted slightly, undoing my bra and letting the material hit the bed, not caring quite where it landed. "That's better," I exhaled a soft sigh.

"That it is," Jaxson said, pleased with my decision. His tongue teased me through my panties, finding that sweet spot to make my toes curl.

My eyes slipped shut, my fingers tugged on the bedsheets, curling between my digits as his fingers took their sweet time to glide my last remaining bit of clothing off. His lips and tongue danced over my skin on a warm path down my thigh, inch by inch, until I wore nothing.

I tried to sit up, pulling at him to come closer. What happened to the hard and frantic pace that we'd started? I wanted that, and he'd gone slow and sweet, savoring his time with me.

"You're going to kill me," I muttered, my back arching off the mattress as his kisses trailed higher toward his intended destination.

His breath lingered for a moment before crawling back up my body while his fingers slid down between my thighs, finding my wetness. "Not kill you, just bring you toward the brink multiple times,"

Jaxson whispered before his lips landed on mine once again.

Warm fingers caressed my body, exciting and arousing me while he guided my legs farther apart, climbing above me. My hand moved down his skin, wanting to take him in, touch him, stroke him before guiding him inside of me.

Slowly, his warmth, his body, became one with mine. I lifted my hips and wrapped my legs around him, guiding him farther and deeper, my back arching off the mattress. Everything fit perfectly.

I clung to him and a flood of warmth tingled within my body. My toes curled, and my insides spasmed.

"I'm going to—"

I didn't let him go, our bodies one. It was too good, too intense, and I didn't have to worry. "You'd better," I muttered into his ear, nipping the lobe before finally letting go, collapsing against the mattress, gasping for air.

He shuddered and grunted the last few strokes, falling against me before rolling onto his side, catching his breath.

A long silence fell over us, our breathing hard, hearts racing in unison.

My eyes fell shut, and the comfort from a warm blanket pulled up and draped over my naked form lulled me toward sleep.

I wanted to say something, but the words didn't come.

Sleep cocooned me, and after the exhausting day earlier, I was out cold.

———

I rolled over in bed, my arm snaked out, finding the mattress beside me cold. I was alone.

"Jaxson?" I mumbled and rubbed the sleep from my tired eyes.

He didn't answer me. No one answered.

Irritated, I sat up in bed, discovering I was indeed naked and hadn't dreamed the previous night.

Sighing, I didn't know why he left, but it didn't matter. If he wanted this to be nothing more than a one-night stand, I could handle that responsibility. I had told him from the beginning that I wasn't looking for a commitment or a relationship.

Begrudgingly, I pushed myself out of bed.

"Shit!" I cursed, glancing at the battery-operated clock on my bedside table. My alarm hadn't gone off.

If I didn't high-tail my ass out of the house soon, I would be late for work. I stumbled through the house, half asleep, pulling a fresh change of clothes on and skipping coffee. There would be coffee at the resort, and I could grab a hot cup when I got to work.

Tossing clothes on, sliding into the warm boots Jaxson gave me, I was hurrying out the door.

I couldn't afford to get a mark on my attendance record or get sacked from my job. The pay wasn't spectacular, but I'd made ends meet over the past month.

My foot was like lead on the gas, swerving down the mountain at a pace I wasn't even comfortable with, and I'd become accustomed to driving back and forth daily.

Every so often, I glanced at the clock, willing time to stop. I knew that was an impossibility, but I hoped that I'd picked up a few minutes on my swift attempt down the mountain.

The only way faster would have been skiing down the slopes, and that wouldn't have ended well for my car or me.

White knuckles gripped the steering wheel. I tried not to think about Jaxson, the heat of his kisses, the taste of his lips, the warmth of his body above mine, overpowering me.

Last night had been amazing, and he'd disappeared after, without a trace.

I'd glanced at my phone before flying off into the car. He hadn't texted. There were no missed calls. I shouldn't have been pissed, but I had the right to feel something.

He'd opened the door to my heart. Trusting didn't come easy, and he bailed the minute after he got what he wanted. Sex.

"Damn him!" I shouted, slamming my hand against the steering wheel.

My heart thudded against my chest. I shifted on the fabric of the seat, hurrying to get to work and anxious for a variety of reasons.

I had to keep what we did a secret. I couldn't tell anyone, least of all Emma.

Hurrying into the parking lot, I slammed on the brakes, the car jolting forward as I came to an abrupt halt. I threw myself out of the car, locked the doors, and with a brisk pace, rushed inside the resort.

The front desk was around the corner, and I barreled inside. Just as I was around the corner, I froze.

I recognized the gentleman from the other day, the one with the leather jacket and baseball hat, an odd combination for the current weather.

Everyone in Breckenridge had thick down jackets, ski coats, or heavy parkas. The black leather didn't look the least bit warm and had to be made for spring.

"I'm sorry, sir. We can't give out information about our guests at the resort," Emma said.

She stood behind the front desk, a plastered smile on her face. Her brow furrowed as she tilted her head slightly to the side.

"I'm not looking for a guest. I believe the woman is an employee and her name is Ariella Ryan."

CHAPTER EIGHTEEN

JAXSON

Last night had been amazing, fantastic, the best night of my life.

No, I wasn't going overboard.

Being with Ariella reminded me how great it was to share the comfort of another and a warm bed.

I hadn't wanted to leave, but my sister, Skylar, had been watching Izzie. Ariella hadn't budged when I kissed her goodbye after throwing my clothes back on. I had scribbled a quick note and left it on her brand-new fridge.

Have to go home to Izzie. I wish I could stay all night with you. Text me if you want me to bring you breakfast. -Jaxson

I had expected she'd text or call. Something to let me know she didn't regret what happened between us and it meant more than a one-night stand to her. I hadn't wanted to seem overzealous with the note or scare her away either.

My phone buzzed on my desk, and I reached out, hopeful that Ariella had answered me.

What time does Izzie go down for a nap?

It was just Skylar.

She had come and visited me unannounced and stayed for the week. I couldn't just bail on my job, and vacation time was usually planned out.

Besides, spending time with my sister was hardly classified as a vacation. At least it kept Izzie from having to go to daycare for the week, which wasn't a bad tradeoff. The daycare always closed by six o'clock, and I was shit for getting there on time. One of the guys would often pick Izzie up if I was stuck in the field on an assignment for a client.

I ignored my sister's text. Izzie would not go down easily for Skylar. She hated naps, and it wasn't even noon yet.

Skylar would have to entertain her all day, not just for a few hours. That was the price for coming to visit.

I was an ass, but if she wanted to spend time with her niece, she needed to act like she wanted to be there.

There were still no messages from Ariella.

Exhaling a heavy sigh, Declan trotted into my office. "We need to have a meeting," Declan said, his arms folded across his chest, his brow tight.

"Sure. What about?"

"Come with me," Declan said, gesturing for me to follow him. His heavy boots trampled on the floor as he led me to the conference room where the rest of the Eagle Tactical team had been situated around the table.

"What's going on? Is there a new assignment?" I asked. Usually, I was consulted with first, but I had been preoccupied lately. Lincoln sat at the table with Declan, Aiden, and Mason.

Lincoln cleared his throat. His expression was grim. "We're worried about your involvement with the new girl." I hadn't expected to see him at Eagle Tactical today.

He was a contractor for us, worked specific assignments when we needed his expertise, but he wasn't a full-time employee because of his restaurant.

Steam shot off my body, and I clenched my fists, my short nails digging into my palm. "My personal life is no one else's business."

I couldn't believe the guys! Were they trying to stage an intervention? They knew I didn't sleep around. I had a daughter to worry about and look after.

Mason leaned back in his chair, all too relaxed for the occasion. "You're getting too close to her, Jaxson. That girl is trouble, forty-two million dollars' worth of trouble."

That had been precisely how much money she'd been charged with stealing. "She's not that girl," I said, defending her. "What her ex-husband did doesn't define her. Besides, don't we all deserve a second chance?"

They'd been through hell.

We all had. We'd carried each other through good times and bad. None of us were free of our burdens and the mistakes that we'd made in the past.

"Listen, I don't know her that well," Lincoln said, "but I saw you two getting pretty cozy in my apartment, and that's not like you. You don't jump headfirst into fucking the hottie next door. That's Aiden's M.O."

My jaw tightened. "You don't know what you're talking about." It was none of their business that we had sex. It wasn't like they could tell!

"I know you're a respectable man," Lincoln said, "but what you were doing wasn't respectable. She'd been drinking. Declan told me you'd been serving her piss-ass drinks at the bar."

It seemed Lincoln hadn't believed me when he'd stumbled into us last night. "I brought her upstairs to have some water, sit down away from the crowd, and calm down. I gave her two drinks earlier that night, and I thought she was having a panic attack after I said something to her downstairs while we were dancing. She has some other medical thing. It doesn't matter," I said, dismissing my rationale.

They didn't need to know about her medical history or what she'd been going through in minute detail.

"Right." Mason didn't believe me.

"I swear she spilled water on my clothes. Nothing happened at your place, Lincoln." I wasn't sleazy like that.

While I may have wanted to rip off her clothes and listen to her scream out my name, I wouldn't have done that on his couch and in his home.

"But something happened?" Lincoln asked.

It wasn't any of their business what transpired between us. We were grown adults, allowed to behave however we chose.

She hadn't been inebriated. It had been two drinks and more time elapsed between her alcohol consumption and when I'd fallen into bed with her

—something that none of them needed to know about.

Aiden sat quietly, his hands folded together on the table. I'd never known him to be so silent. "Do you have anything to add?" I asked.

"I haven't met her," Aiden said. "I've read her file, the one our client asked us to retrieve on her. I rarely agree with mixing business and pleasure, but I've never seen you so happy. Despite that, I don't know her. I only know what's on paper, and the girl has secrets. Did you know what she used to do for a living before her life blew up?"

I hadn't asked her, and after I'd seen the name 'Ariella Ryan' and had realized the connection, there had been no reason for me to continue searching for information. "No, I guess I don't know what she did for a living. Does it matter?"

I hadn't asked her. I should have. I didn't think it mattered.

"Before she was fired, Ariella Ryan was an agent for the C.I.A. She did remote surveillance internationally for several years before she married and settled down in New York City, working at a field office and pretending to be the curator for a small museum."

I held Declan's stare.

Was he serious?

The woman had many secrets but a C.I.A. operative? I couldn't even imagine it was the truth.

She was small, fragile, and while I didn't consider her helpless, I'd seen how she reacted last night and doubted her ability to do any field work.

"You're skeptical," Mason said. "I was too, especially after meeting her, but it makes sense. Why else would she want to live off-grid?"

I shook my head. I didn't believe it.

She'd been upset when she found out the cabin didn't have electricity, angry in fact.

Had she played me?

Declan slid a manila folder across the table at me.

I forced the file open and sifted through the pages quickly to see what was true and what wasn't. "Why didn't this come up when I searched for her name?"

"She goes deep," Mason said. "Her cover was nearly blown by her ex-husband when he was arrested. After that, the details get a little fuzzy, but we suspect her marriage may have been a cover. She went deep, a little too deep, and when the government went after her husband, someone put a target on her back and went after her too."

I ran a hand through my hair. "This all sounds crazy." I had trouble wrapping my head around what they told me, but staring at the file, it was all in there. A copy of her identification and a scan of her C.I.A. credentials, including her badge. "Are you sure this is her?"

"It gets worse," Mason said. "We've been doing a lot of digging into her past. From what we can surmise, her husband may not have been responsible for the Ponzi scheme he went to prison for last year. She's still being hunted by the same men who set up her husband. From what I found on the dark web, there's a hit for Ariella Ryan, aka Ariella Cole."

Fear crept into my chest, suffocating me. She was in danger.

"The good news is her exact location hasn't been discovered yet," Aiden said. "We still have time to help her if that's what you want."

I stood, the file open but forgotten on the conference table. "Of course, it's what I want. She needs our help. If she's C.I.A., then she's practically one of us."

"I'm not sure I'd go that far," Lincoln retorted, his tone sharp, his eyes tight. He didn't seem on board with helping her.

Even if she weren't C.I.A. and had just been a girl with a self-destructive past, I still would have helped her.

I wasn't keen on the fact she'd lied to me, kept the truth from me, but she needed my help.

I wasn't going to abandon her when shit got tough.

My phone buzzed in my pocket. "I swear if it's Skylar again," I grunted under my breath and withdrew my cell phone.

I held up a finger to tell the guys to hold on a minute. "It's Ariella," I said.

My stomach twisted like a vine, worry evident on my face. I swallowed the rising lump in my throat and planted my feet firm on the floor to ground myself. I had plenty of practice in the field, not letting my emotions overcome me. Today was no different.

I needed to be strong for Ariella, and as pissed as I was that she lied to me, I also needed to keep a level head. I didn't want her turning her back on me now, not after what we shared last night.

"Go on, answer it." Mason gestured to my phone.

The guys would not give me an ounce of privacy, but I deserved that after having my head shoved in the sand, unaware of the truth of her past and the danger that surrounded all of us.

"Hello?" I didn't get another word out before her words poured out of her in a whisper.

"It's Ariella. I need your help. There's someone at the resort looking for me, and they're using my married name. Can you pull surveillance from the hotel and find out who it is?"

She certainly knew a lot about what we could do, Eagle Tactical's capabilities, without a warrant.

A typical citizen wouldn't have been so knowledgeable, but a C.I.A. agent would know our skills and abilities to do what she asked.

"Are you in danger?" I asked, not answering her question.

She still didn't know that I was aware of her previous career, her life before she was married, the secret she'd kept from me.

Was I mad at her for deceiving me? Yes, but I would not let that cloud my judgment when she needed my help.

"I don't know," she whispered. "Possibly. I'm hoping it's just someone after me because of what Benjamin stole."

"Ariella, we need to talk, clear the air about some things." I stood, unable to just sit and listen to what she said. I put the phone on speaker.

"I know," she stammered. "Shit. He's coming this direction."

"Describe him to me." I muted her call. "She's at Blue Sky Resort. We need immediate access to the surveillance footage. I recall that we set up their system and it's all backed up to the cloud."

Declan pushed himself up, the chair squeaking as he stood. "I'll work on getting backdoor access. As soon as I get his name, I'll have Mason run a background on the guy."

"I want to know if he so much as has a parking ticket in his name," I said.

"Of course," Declan said.

Mason's expression remained grim, but he didn't speak.

I unmuted the call and tried to catch up with what Ariella had said about the man's description.

Lincoln had jotted it all down while we'd talked amongst each other, and I glanced over the list describing his height, weight, hair color, and clothes.

"I found it odd he was wearing a leather jacket when there was snow on the ground. It caught my attention, but I didn't recognize him," Ariella said. "He was outside in the parking lot when I left work yesterday evening. I almost walked by him at the front desk when he spoke to Emma."

"Mason and Declan are giving me a hand with getting access to the surveillance footage and running background on this mystery man. I'm going to head out to the resort with Lincoln and pick you up. Can you lie low, find someplace to hide? We will text you when we're at the resort."

A muffled gasp erupted from the opposite end of the line.

My heart dropped into my stomach.

I snatched my phone from the conference table and shrugged my coat on as I rushed out to my truck.

Heavy steps followed me with Lincoln on my heels while he tried to catch up. I hadn't exactly announced I was leaving right now, but with the sound of a struggle, I couldn't wait another moment.

"Ariella?" I pulled the keys from my pocket, started the engine, and rushed outside into the brisk chill.

Evidence of a struggle, a gasp, a clack, something had fallen.

Was it the phone?

The line went dead.

CHAPTER NINETEEN

ARIELLA

Sweaty, rough hands snatched me from the hiding space in the hallway.

My phone fell to the ground, and the assailant stepped down with his boots, smashing my device to pieces, crunching the screen under his steel-toed boots.

I hadn't expected anyone to come from behind, not when the man with the baseball cap had been just a few feet away, around the corner, in front of me.

I had kept hidden.

Little good it did me. My defensive tactical training kicked in.

My years at the C.I.A. had involved hands-on combat training even though I was practically a desk clerk with a background in technology, science, and profiling. The only fieldwork I had done was surveillance assignments, a side effect of my health issues that had occurred early in my career but after passing all required training and tests. Lucky me.

He restrained my neck in a headlock, keeping me from breathing, I had seconds before I would go unconscious.

I slammed my elbow into the assailant's groin, smashed my head back into his nose, and spun around to escape his grip around my neck.

Gasping hard, trying to drink in all the oxygen that I could, my heart screamed for help, but the words never left my lips.

I didn't recognize the blond, beady-eyed man. His thick muscles protruded from his t-shirt.

"Connor. She's over here!"

Connor?

He must have been the one with that stupid baseball cap who was asking about me. I didn't recognize the man's name, and the beady-eyed attacker was a stranger to me as well.

Connor, the man with the baseball cap, strolled around the corner. His footsteps were thudding against the tile floor, coming toward me, blocking off my exit out of the hallway.

"What do you want?" Had it been the money Benjamin stole, or were they after me because I had once worked for the C.I.A.?

Had my identity been leaked by my previous employer or someone else?

I had no access to state secrets, no special privileges as a former agent. I was a disgrace to the agency, and they'd make that clear when I had been forced to resign.

Yanking on my long dark hair, the beady-eyed man took a fistful into his palm, gripping the strands. He tugged hard.

I screamed from the pain while he dragged me out the back hall to the exit.

Screaming for help, I kicked and dug my toes into the stone road, but it didn't help.

I tried twisting to break free, but he moved fast, my hair tangled in his grip.

Connor was in front of me, a switchblade in his hand. The cold steel grazed my cheek. "Scared yet?" he seethed between crooked teeth as his partner held me captive.

"Let me go!" I struggled against him and fought back with every ounce of strength I could muster.

My elbow jammed into his stomach.

He chucked me against the icy brick exterior of the building.

My head smacked the rough texture before my legs buckled beneath me.

"We know who you are," Connor said, kicking my chest, knocking the wind out of me again. "We want our investment returned to us. All two million dollars, and since we're generous, we'll only tack on another two million in interest. You'll get it to us by sundown tonight."

I snorted under my breath. It had to be dirty money.

What the hell had Benjamin been thinking when he'd taken their money to invest and steal? Two million wasn't a small amount, and they wanted four million by sundown?

Beady-eyed man held me down, his weight pinning me to the ground, his arms overpowering me, while Connor brought the blade against my skin.

Laughing, he tore at my coat, ripping my warmth to shreds. The edge scratched my skin and tore at my clothes.

A fire burned over my arms and chest. I fought back with my forearms, struggling to get up, and while I tried to roll him over, having two men made it an impossible match.

The longer I stayed down, the easier it was for them to continue to attack me.

My fingers grazed over the stone pavement. I slipped a rock into my palm, prepared to use it to defend myself.

Connor released his grip, closed the switchblade, and shoved it into his back pocket.

A heavy snort left beady-eye's lips, and with only one man and no weapon against my skin, I swung my hips and thrust my body around, using my legs to kick his legs out from under him, forcing him onto his back as I pinned him down and smacked him with the rock.

"Never touch me again," I snarled, breathing, heavy anger chilling me along with the cold.

Connor reached down, offering a hand to his buddy to help him up. "Four million, or you'll be digging a grave for the little girl and her daddy."

How did they know about Jaxson and Izzie?

I held my breath for a few seconds before exhaling a slow and even lungful.

How long had they been watching me? Since the day I moved into the cabin?

I hadn't seen Izzie in over a month. Jaxson and I hadn't been close again until last night.

The world spun around me. I leaned back against the cold, rough brick of the building and let it support my weight and my shaky legs.

"I'll get you the money." I gritted my teeth, and a toughness washed over me.

I didn't know how I would save them.

I didn't have four million dollars, but I would let nothing happen to either of them. "Where is the drop?" I asked.

———

I stood outside with a torn jacket, shivering by the front entrance.

I walked from the back exit, where I'd been threatened and beaten, to the main doors. I threw away my shredded coat, the bloodstains a reminder of my weakness.

I didn't even know where I bled from. Everything ached, and the cuts where the blade had gashed my skin burned, but I hadn't seen any significant injuries.

Waiting for Jaxson, time appeared to stand still.

Shivering, I stood in my torn pale pink sweater. It was too thin for winter, and my jacket was worthless, as was the sweater I wore, but that wasn't hitting the trash until I got home.

His dark blue truck tore into the parking lot and came to an abrupt halt in front of the resort.

Jaxson left the truck running before he leaped out of the vehicle.

Lincoln sat in the passenger seat, his expression gruff. He didn't look pleased to see me or to have his day interrupted.

Jaxson hurried around to me, removing his coat and pulling it on my shoulders.

He opened the back door and helped me into his truck. The warmth of his jacket and the heat surrounded me.

"Thanks," I said. My shoulders trembled as I shivered in the truck.

Jaxson scooted into the backseat beside me and shut the truck door.

There was nowhere to move, with our proximity tight, and his knees brushed up against my legs. His warm hand grazed my cheek, and the other tangled in my hair, glancing me over from head to toe.

Unlike the men who had attacked me, Jaxson's touch was gentle yet firm.

I grimaced. My head ached from when I'd been slammed into the brick wall.

"I'll drive us to the hospital," Lincoln said and scooted over to the driver's side.

"That's unnecessary." I didn't want to go to the hospital.

There would be too many questions, and the police would have me file a report, and an investigation would be underway. "I can't go to the hospital. Isn't it two hours from here?"

"A little less than that," Jaxson answered.

He leaned forward and retrieved a tin box labeled 'first aid' from beneath the passenger seat.

"I'm all right," I said as he tended to the wound on my head.

He took a penlight from his kit and had me follow the light with my eyes.

"Since when did you become a medic?" I asked.

His expression remained blank, and he shut off the light. "She doesn't appear to have a concussion. Why don't you drive us back to Eagle Tactical?" Jaxson asked. He turned his attention back to me. "Since when did you become a C.I.A. operative?" he retorted.

I winced and swallowed the lump in my throat. "How did you know?"

No one was supposed to find that out. I had been assured that my identity and past with the agency had been scrubbed clean.

Jaxson didn't answer my question. "What happened in there?"

I rubbed the back of my neck and shrugged off his coat.

Was it warm in the truck or was I feverish under his scrutiny?

He pulled his coat tighter around my shoulders. The coat was warm around my shoulders, and I slipped my arms into the sleeves. Jaxson fastened the zipper, pulling it to the top. "You're freezing, Freckles. You need this more than I do."

Hearing the name he'd given me made me warm and toasty. "I don't feel cold," I whispered. My eyes fell to his lap.

He opened an alcohol wipe and swiped it against the abrasion on my forehead.

I hissed from the sting that radiated through my head. "Tell me you have drugs in there."

While I appreciated him taking care of me, I didn't like the burning sensation that the alcohol caused.

"There might be a few ibuprofen," Jaxson said. He tended to the gash on my head, cleaning it before using butterfly bandages to close the wound. "There's nothing any stronger if that's what you're asking."

He leaned forward and kissed my injury when he was done.

Lincoln's eyes were on us as he drove, every so often glancing in the rearview mirror. I did not know what he thought of me. I wasn't sure I wanted to know.

The look of loathing was enough to send my heart plummeting.

I told Jaxson everything about Connor and the man with the baseball cap, how they'd attacked me and demanded four million dollars by sunset. While I hadn't wanted to tell him the rest, he deserved to know the truth and hear it from me.

"They'd been watching me, probably since the day I came to town. They knew about you and Izzie," I said.

Jaxson closed up the first aid kit and shoved it back under the seat.

His hand latched onto mine. While I'd always known his hands were large, the warmth eased my anxiety a little.

"They threatened you," he said, matter of fact, like my life hadn't just been torn apart and blown up in one afternoon.

I winced when I attempted a nod. "Yes. I'm so sorry." I didn't want him to hate me.

While I wasn't keen on Lincoln's intolerable glare, I didn't want to experience that from Jaxson.

He lifted his hips and retrieved his phone from his pocket. "Skylar, it's Jaxson. I need you to make sure the doors are locked and keep Izzie inside and away from any windows. Arm the alarm and then take her into the playroom. Don't answer the door for anyone, is that clear?"

He hung up his phone and shoved the device back into his pocket. "Head straight for my place," Jaxson said.

"Affirmative," Lincoln said.

Lincoln had downshifted the truck and rolled out the gears, he hurried up the mountain pass to get to Jaxson's house quicker. The pace quickened as trees whizzed by the windows on our way up.

I didn't know what we would do about the men or the money that they wanted, but they were becoming two thoughts furthest from my mind.

I was worried about Izzie. Jaxson's hands gave mine a tentative squeeze.

He was concerned too.

"I'm sorry," I said, keeping my voice low, so the conversation was between the two of us.

A stony stare from Lincoln made my heart skip a beat, and I met his gaze in the rearview mirror.

Jaxson's jaw remained tight, his shoulders square. "I have to ask you something and you owe me the respect of answering honestly."

I wanted to tell him I'd always been honest, and while I'd kept secrets, I hadn't lied to him, not outright.

My stomach bubbled with fear and dread.

What was he going to ask now?

I gave him the best smile I could muster to ease any worries that he had and squeezed his hands in mine. "Of course. What is it?"

"When you moved into the cabin the very first night, you told me you were shocked about not having electricity. Did you lie to me? The more I play that night over in my head. I keep thinking that you genuinely seemed surprised but knowing what I do, that you wanted to move off-grid, go somewhere that you wouldn't be exposed, it makes sense that you would have intended not to have electric."

Jaxson unclasped his hold from me and dug out his phone again. He pulled up the original listing on the cabin. He showed me the listing, holding his phone for me to see.

Off-grid. Quiet, rustic living at its finest either year-round or the perfect getaway cabin with hundreds of miles of trails all around.

"I hadn't taken off-grid to mean no electricity."

"Well, you should have," Lincoln added sharply from the driver's seat.

I pursed my lips, considering the right words. Why was he pissed at me?

Was it because I had worked for the agency or because he was defending his friend? "Yes, off-grid could mean no electric, but it can also mean a small town in the middle of nowhere which is precisely what the cabin is and where it's located."

I'd spent a great deal of time looking into small towns, but most I hadn't been capable of affording, and getting a loan would have been too risky. I needed to keep a low profile, little good that had done.

I'd still been found, and I wasn't sure where I'd messed up, except my credit card. While it had been assigned to my maiden name, the name I'd legally taken, it was possible some asshat had figured that out and exposed me.

Now they were hunting me down.

"Shit."

"What?" Jaxson asked.

He shoved his phone back into his pocket. We turned off the road, onto the last trail up to his house in the woods.

"I just realized how they found me. I've been stupid. I thought that if I kept a low profile, everything would blow over, but it's clear that was a mistake."

"You've made a lot of mistakes," Lincoln muttered from the front seat.

"What's that?" I shot back and turned to face him, letting go of any trace of Jaxson against me.

The truck came to an abrupt halt. "We're here," Lincoln said, putting the truck in park.

"Stay in the truck. Keep the doors locked."

Lincoln shut off the engine and took the keys with him. They locked the truck and hurried inside.

"How am I supposed to stay warm?" I asked.

No one could hear me. Both men were already outside rushing to get into the house and make sure Izzie was all right.

A red hatchback sat in the driveway in front of the house. I didn't recognize the car, but I hadn't been to his house. I shifted closer to the door but kept inside the vehicle.

The truck's engine roared to life, and I jumped in my seat, realizing Jaxson had turned on the auto start. At least I wouldn't freeze to death.

Part of me wanted to help. I didn't enjoy sitting around, watching events unfold and not being involved. I also knew I was no good if I was injured, and I didn't have the luxury of acting like an agent, gun drawn, running around with body armor.

The reality was I never had a traditional field assignment unless you called stakeouts and surveillance operations exciting. It wasn't a thrilling job, but it was essential in catching the bad guys.

I missed being able to use my skills. The resort hadn't been the most exciting job, but I thought it would have given me a fresh start. Instead, it paid barely above minimum wage, and I'd been tracked down. That wasn't anyone at the resort's fault.

I was prone to keeping secrets. That's all I'd ever known but look what good it had done.

I had lied to Jaxson, the one guy I liked and had a chance with, all because telling the truth was too hard and too risky. I was worried about being exposed and look where that got me.

I hated myself.

BOOM!

BOOM!

A loud explosion rattled the truck and blew out the windows.

I covered my ears and my head on instinct, but I heard nothing but a slight ringing sensation and beyond that, silence.

CHAPTER TWENTY

JAXSON

Jogging into the house, key in hand, I threw open the door and unarmed the alarm, leaving the door wide open behind me for Lincoln to follow.

I didn't turn around to see where he was. I didn't wait for him.

"Skylar! Izzie!" I shouted and hurried through the house, upstairs to the playroom, where I told them to go.

I threw open the door and lunged inside, only to find it empty.

"Skylar! Izzie!" I tried again, hoping they would answer me, needing to know they were both all right.

Isabella was my world, and while Skylar wasn't my favorite person, I trusted her to look after Izzie and make sure she was safe.

Silence filled the house as I flung each door open, searching high and low for both of them.

I fled down the stairs and to the basement, discovering Izzie in a laundry bin atop a mound of bedsheets.

Skylar had the lid of the dryer open doing a load of darks. The washing machine tumbled and thudded, probably making it difficult to hear, besides the basement's soundproofing. I had set it up as a training facility before we invested in the building that we have now for Eagle Tactical.

I exhaled a sigh of relief, throwing my arms around Izzie, pulling her tight and spinning her around, comforted that she was safe.

"Sorry, I didn't hear you guys come in." Skylar glanced at me over her shoulder and pointed at

Lincoln. "We haven't met," she said, smiling and putting out her hand for an introduction.

"I'm Lincoln Taylor." He offered his hand. "It's a pleasure to meet you." Lincoln smiled charmingly at my sister and brought her hand to his lips.

Skylar grinned and giggled. It didn't take a genius to see what was happening between the two of them.

"She's off-limits." I wanted it made clear that he wasn't to date Skylar.

If they dated, then I'd have to see more of her. That was the last thing I wanted, for Skylar to find another reason to hang around Breckenridge.

There were other reasons, too.

She was far too juvenile to handle Lincoln.

She liked to play the field and go out partying. I was lucky she hadn't done that in town, coming home after the bar closed, trashed, and stumbling through the front door.

I wouldn't tolerate that type of behavior, certainly not around Izzie.

BOOM!

The house vibrated from a nearby explosion. I clutched Izzie to my chest, covering her, uncertain what was happening around us.

Lincoln met my stare. I handed Izzie back to Skylar. "Stay down here." My boots smacked the stairs hard on the way up, running out the front door to check on Ariella.

The truck's window had been shattered. I ran through the snow to the truck, my feet slipping under me, but I caught myself before falling. "Ariella?"

Her head poked up, her eyes wide and her body trembling.

"I was just sitting here when the windows blew. It sounded like an explosion nearby."

No one could have missed the deafening roar.

"Do you smell that?" she asked.

I spun around, glancing over my shoulder toward the bridge between our houses. Smoke billowed into the sky.

Ariella unlatched the door and yanked it open. I took a step back, getting out of the way for her. Her feet sunk into the snow with each quick step she took toward the bridge.

Unlike at the house, where I'd shoveled and it had slightly iced over, the bridge's path was thick with recent wet snow.

"Stay with Skylar," I shouted at Lincoln as he stood on the porch, his brow furrowed and phone in his hand. He pointed in the smoke's direction. He saw it now, too.

"I'm calling the fire department," Lincoln said.

I followed Ariella through the forest and across the bridge, along the trail between our properties. It was much shorter and a quicker route than by truck.

Thick, black smoke rose into the chilly air. The heat of the fire roared and whipped with the wind against the cabin. There was no chance of saving it or anything inside.

"No!" Ariella shouted, rushing toward the cabin.

I hurried after her, grabbing her by the waist, restraining her as she tried to break free, twisting and turning to pull herself from my grasp.

"Please! I have to get inside!"

"You can't," I whispered against her ear, clinging to her body, holding her back, willing her to stay with me.

Didn't she understand the danger?

The fire bellowed and boomed, the sound deafening as it ate away at the structure, fire soaring outside through the windows and where the roof had been moments earlier.

Her body went limp in my arms, and I scooped her up and carried her back to my house.

"Put me down!" She tried to pry out of my embrace and eventually gave in when I didn't let her go. Her head rested against my chest, her arms around my neck.

"Is she okay?" Lincoln opened the front door for me as I brought her inside and gently guided her onto the sofa to lie down.

"I'm fine," Ariella said, sitting up, her feet dangling off the sofa instead of stretched out like I'd laid her.

She unzipped my coat and pulled it off, handing it to me.

"What was so important in that house that you felt it necessary to run into burning flames? I know you don't have a pet, and no one else lives there." I'd been there the night before, and it had just been the two of us, alone, exploring each other's bodies.

Already, it seemed like a lifetime ago.

She hadn't even acknowledged my letter that I'd left her on the fridge. All that would have to wait. There were more pressing matters at hand. Besides, I wasn't even sure I could forgive her yet and be with someone who had deceived me.

I pushed the memories from last night away. I had to compartmentalize what happened between us.

"In my knapsack, there were some photos." Her eyes were cast down toward the floor.

I stepped closer and bent down. "What kind of photos?"

I wasn't able to ignore the knot in my stomach. She found it necessary to lie to me again.

What had she hidden away in the cabin that was worth risking her life over?

"You wouldn't understand." Her piercing green eyes glanced up at me.

"Try me, Freckles." I kept her trapped against the sofa. My legs straddled hers.

She swallowed, and her tongue darted out, licking her lips. Silence enveloped the room.

"I'm going to check on Skylar and Isabella," Lincoln said. He hustled out of the room and down the basement stairs.

Each thud was louder than the previous against the wooden steps.

Ariella gnawed on her bottom lip, tugging the cherry pink edge between her teeth. Her eyes fell to the floor.

"You *will* answer me, Freckles." I lifted her chin with my thumb, my fingers grazing her tender skin.

"What was the question?" Her lips pouted, her brow furrowed, and she tilted her head to the side.

"You are the queen of avoidance, aren't you?" I could see it written all over her face. "Don't play me." I didn't like games, and I would not engage in them with her. "The photographs in your cabin. What are they? Family photos? Something else? It's just you and me. You owe me an honest answer, Ariella. Especially after you lied to me about why you came to Breckenridge."

A soft puff of air escaped her lips with a sigh. She gently pushed against my chest. When I didn't move out of her way, she rolled her eyes and folded her arms against her chest. "It wasn't a lie. I've never told anyone who I used to work for, even when they employed me."

"You mean the C.I.A.," I said. Even now, she avoided using the agency's name.

Ariella shifted against the sofa but couldn't move farther than her butt allowed without sweeping her legs away from me, which she didn't do.

I reached out and guided her arms from their folded position. Taking her hands in mine, I could feel that her fingers were frigid from the outside temperature. Her cheeks also had a slight blush which I assumed had been from the cold. It could have also resulted from the stress of her home burning down to the ground.

"You're freezing. Why didn't you say anything?"

"It didn't seem important," she whispered, meeting my stare.

On the back of the leather sofa rested a throw blanket.

I stood and pulled the warm blanket down and unfolded the Sherpa, covering her with it. Her shoulders slumped, and her demeanor seemed to relax once she was tight under the blanket. I sat beside her, my legs brushing against hers, sitting atop the blanket.

"You need to take better care of yourself. I understand you're upset about the fire, but whatever was destroyed, it wasn't worth dying over."

"You don't know that," Ariella said, her eyes wide. She turned to face me. Her hands clutched the blanket around her small frame.

"Then explain it to me." I didn't enjoy being left in the dark. She continually gave me pieces of a puzzle, one at a time. "I don't like being strung along or having to drag secrets out of someone."

She trembled beneath the blanket, and I couldn't tell if it resulted from her being chilled or the adrenaline issues that she'd had the previous day.

Was this a daily occurrence regarding her health? Another question that I wanted answers to but wasn't expecting all of it explained tonight. Foremost, was the lie about her past, the fact she'd worked for the C.I.A., and whatever had her risking her life to go back inside for that stupid knapsack.

"About four years ago, I was pregnant," Ariella said.

Pacing the length of the living room, I could have easily worn a hole through the floor. Restless energy poured out of me until I heard her faint answer.

That took me by surprise. I swallowed the lump in the back of my throat. "I didn't know." I didn't want to overwhelm her. Approaching her, I towered above. "What happened?"

She stared down at the blanket. "Noah was born prematurely, at twenty-eight weeks. There were complications for both the baby and for me. He was a fighter, lived two weeks in NICU but in the end, it was just too much."

I sat down beside her, my hand falling on her thigh, giving her a reassuring squeeze. "I'm so sorry."

My heart ached.

Her son would have been around the same age as Izzie. It broke my heart to imagine what she went through and experienced.

She pressed her lips tight. "Me too. The fire took the last and only picture I had of my son."

Heaviness weighed over me.

Her eyes glistened with tears and she breathed in, sniffling, but the wetness didn't fall from her eyes.

Her strength surpassed mine.

"I don't want to talk about it anymore. It hurts too much to think about. I miss him every day, but his hospital bracelet and photo were inside my knapsack."

I pulled her into my lap, my embrace crushing her, keeping her tight to me.

Her body trembled. Her breaths were shallow and short.

"Let me take your pain away," I whispered into her ear.

Her cheeks were flushed. Her hands came up to my neck, icy cold. She ran her fingers through my hair. "You can't. No one can."

My forehead pressed firmly against hers. I wouldn't take that as an answer. I wanted to lay her down on the sofa and kiss her pain away.

"I don't know how I would have raised Noah with Benjamin in prison, on my own." Ariella winced. "I'm sorry."

"About what?" Why was she apologizing to me?

She kissed my cheek before she moved her head to rest on my shoulder. "I don't know how you do it." She paused for a beat, exhaling a heavy sigh. "Raise a daughter by yourself. It's impressive to me that you're a single father and you work full-time."

"Maybe it will comfort you to know that we believe you and your ex-husband were set up," I said.

She pulled back from my embrace. I thought hearing that would have made her happy. "What?"

"Blue Sky Resort requested that we run a background check on you before you were hired. I didn't dig too deep. Once I connected you were married to Benjamin Ryan, I'll admit, I lost my shit."

"Is that an apology?" Ariella asked, tilting her head before climbing off my lap. I didn't want her to pull away.

"It might be," I said. "Mason kept digging and discovered your previous employer. There were a number of questionable transactions that were traced back to the C.I.A.. Mason brought up that someone might have set you and Benjamin up."

"Who would set him up? Unless they were also setting me up, but why? Could there be a mole in the organization, someone who set me up to take the fall?" Rubbing her temples, she leaned forward, her head in her hands.

I hoped she wasn't about to get sick. I wanted to take her back with me to Eagle Tactical, but I wasn't sure she'd be willing to go.

The anger quelled and dissipated as her body relaxed. "I never thought I would want to thank Mason," she said.

"You'll have your chance."

"Benjamin wasn't guilty?" Her voice was soft, reflective of the news. "He's serving a 150-year term in federal prison for securities fraud, wire fraud, money laundering, the list goes on. Gosh, I'm such an asshole." She pulled away from my touch. "I told him I hated him, that I never wanted to see him or talk to him again."

I hadn't considered the fact she might still have harbored feelings for her ex-husband. If he wasn't guilty, what chance did I have that she'd even want to be with me?

I ran a hand through my short hair and needed to change the subject fast. The whole thought of Ariella feeling guilty and wanting to be with him again made bile rise into my throat.

"That aside," I said and cleared my throat. "We have more pressing matters. You mentioned earlier that the thugs who attacked you demanded four million dollars."

"That's right. I don't have that kind of money. If I did, do you think I'd be living in the woods without electricity or accessible heat?"

She had accessible heat. It may not have been the easiest method to warm the place, but the cabin still could be kept plenty warm. I held my tongue. There was no sense fighting over a cabin that had burned to the ground. The fire department would take at least twenty minutes to climb the mountain, and whatever water the truck had would be all they could use.

Twenty minutes was too long to save the cabin, but it would stop the destruction from spreading and turning the forest into a giant tinder box.

The wail of sirens on their approach echoed outside and through the canopy of trees.

"I don't have that kind of money, either, but I think there's another way." I headed for the window, staring outside at the heavy blackness, like clouds that billowed to the sky, for a moment before turning around to give her my attention.

Ariella stood slowly, folding the blanket back to its original shape, each corner perfectly lined up to match. "I would love nothing more than never to lay eyes on those men again, but I know if we don't stop them, next time will be worse."

She placed the Sherpa blanket over the back of the sofa where I'd grabbed it from earlier. "Do you think they're somehow responsible for the fire?" she asked.

Ariella walked ever so quietly. Her footsteps were silent to the ear. Had I not been watching from the corner of my eye, I never would have known she stood beside me.

I turned and watched the plume of smoke.

"Can we go outside and watch?" Her voice was soft and tentative. Was she afraid I'd tell her no?

While I wasn't keen on taking her with me, I wanted to survey the scene and determine if evidence had been left behind out in the open. If the firemen hadn't arrived yet, maybe we could spot tire tracks or footprints.

Years of tactical and military training told me this wasn't an accident. It was risky but I wasn't going to let anything happen to Ariella.

"Take this," I said and offered her my coat, the same one she'd worn earlier. I grabbed another jacket to put on.

"Wait here. Let me tell Lincoln what we're doing so he doesn't worry." I hurried down the basement steps, informed Lincoln and Skylar that we would check out the fire next door and see if anything suspicious stood out.

"That was fast."

I had little to tell them, and I didn't want Ariella going alone. I opened the front door and led her outside. "It's hard to say, but if I trust my gut, they won't be too far from here."

If someone had intentionally started the fire, they'd have stuck around watching the damage they caused.

With my hand on the small of her back, I led her through the forest and across the bridge.

Smiling, she still wore the boots I'd given her. I bought them as a gift for my sister when she visited and never brought sensible shoes. The box had been shucked in the back of my closet and now had finally seen the light of day.

We crossed the bridge. Through the tree line, red lights flickered and flashed from the fire engine pulling into the driveway of her property.

She grumbled under her breath. "Would you look at that? The damned shed survived."

The structure had been on its last legs. It was any wonder the thick smoke hadn't knocked the building over.

"I guess I know where I'll be living from now on," she muttered and shoved her hands into her coat pockets.

There was no chance in hell I'd let her live in that crooked shed. "What about insurance money for the cabin?"

Insurance would pay to rebuild the house and her living expenses up to a certain amount, depending on her coverage.

The firefighters unlatched the hose and used the reservoir of water available. There weren't any fire hydrants nearby.

Water blasted the fire, causing a thicket of smoke to flood the area. I reached out, grabbing Ariella against me, and ducked my head into my jacket to breathe.

The outside air burned my lungs.

She coughed on the plumes as the wind shifted direction toward us while we stood behind the property. "I don't have insurance," she choked out.

The flames had been suffocated by water, smothering us in the process as the breeze picked up.

The gust of air brought the charred remnants ablaze, ash in the air, embers floating like fireflies gliding in the wind. My eyes burned, and Ariella continued to cough on the smoke.

We needed to turn around. This had been stupid and dangerous. I'd thrown her right into danger.

The heaviness of the air filled with dark smoke turned me around. The bridge wasn't visible. With one arm around her waist, I pulled her through the dense fog of smoke. I couldn't even see my own hands in front of me.

I held my breath and pulled her tight against me so that she wouldn't get lost and wander into further danger. Smoke burned my eyes. My nose tickled from the ash. This was my fault.

The breeze picked up, and I gasped, needing a drink of air into my lungs. Ariella coughed and wheezed, the smoke bothering her far worse. The air caught beneath the charred remnants of the cabin, and the fire blazed back to life as we grew too close in the smoke to see.

Heat sizzled against my cheeks.

I cursed and yanked Ariella closer, pulling her behind me. "Keep your arms around my waist," I demanded.

I needed my hands to feel my way through the trees and while I didn't want to get burned, I wanted even less for her to be the one to discover the wild flames.

Skirting the fire, a blast of wetness smothered the flames momentarily. More smoke charged into the air.

I coughed and stumbled forward.

My eyes burned.

Through the heat and warmth that had been nearby, still simmering on the foundation, I led us around the property. Sweat coated my cheeks and brow while my back pebbled with goosebumps from the chill.

Bringing her with me around the fire and away from the smoke, escaping harm's way, I sensed the brightness before seeing anything clear. My vision blurred from the smoke, but one foot smacked the ground in front of the other.

Panting hard, I collapsed forward, away from the plumes of smoke, my knees on the icy cold snow, breathing in the fresh air—the smoke behind us.

I heard the shouts of firefighters. I was no good to Ariella.

My hands clutched the earth, gasping hard for each breath of oxygen that I could.

With blurred eyes, a man towered above me.

A mask covered my lips and my vision wavered and blurred before the world went black.

CHAPTER TWENTY-ONE

ARIELLA

"Jaxson?" He'd stumbled forward, one foot and then another until he'd fallen onto his knees.

I crouched down, keeping him close.

"Help!" I shouted for the firefighters, hoping there was a paramedic nearby. My hands clutched his jacket, and my fingers stroked his hair. I didn't see any burn marks, no evidence of injuries.

Unless it was something I couldn't see, perhaps smoke inhalation. Could it be something else that I didn't know about? "Please, help him!"

The smack of boots against the snow forced a shiver down my spine and my hair to stand on end. It reminded me of glass crunching underfoot. A team of paramedics rushed over to help.

Jaxson's body went slack, but my hands caught him before he hit his face into the snow, guiding him down as gracefully as I could.

I coughed and gasped. Waves of dizziness washed over me, but I ignored the spinning sensation.

Jaxson needed help.

I could wait. I would wait because he was in need. He had a daughter, and if something happened to him because of my carelessness, I would never forgive myself.

One paramedic gently guided me away, informing me they needed space. I didn't want to let go of his hand; I didn't want to lose the only connection I had with someone. Letting go was not an answer I would accept.

"No," I shook my head repeatedly, trembling, although I wasn't cold.

Nausea attacked my stomach, and I pushed a wayward lock of hair behind my ear, exhaling through my mouth. Anything to keep from spilling my lunch. Except, I couldn't remember the last time I ate.

My head throbbed, my heart pounded, and my stomach coiled. "I won't leave him," I said, clutching his hand tight. "He didn't leave me."

"We need to look you over," the gentleman said, his eyes studying the bump I sustained earlier. "You should get checked out too."

"I'm not going anywhere without Jaxson." I refused to release my grip on his hand. No one would separate us.

The paramedic grumbled and gave a resigned sigh. "Well, would you at least have a seat so I can check you out too? I'm worried about the injury to your head."

He hadn't even seen all the cuts and bruises, the scrapes that covered me from earlier.

"I'm fine," I insisted, pointing at the bandage on my head. "This is unrelated." I squatted with my knees bent, keeping a close eye on Jaxson, ignoring the attention that the paramedic paid to me.

"Yes, and you're bleeding right through your bandage," the paramedic said. He grabbed a few pads of gauze in a nearby bag with gloved hands and rested it against my forehead.

I winced from the initial sting of contact. There were droplets of fresh blood in the snow—my blood.

My butt slumped into the cold, slushy snow.

My gloved hand rubbed over the evidence of my blood, burying it from anyone else's watchful gaze.

"Why don't you come with me? Sit in the back of the ambulance bay so I can patch up your head," the paramedic said.

Another paramedic tended to Jaxson, covering his face with an oxygen mask against his mouth and nose.

"Will he be all right?"

The paramedic escorted me through the snow and wet sludge to the bay of the ambulance. He yanked open the double doors and offered me a hand, helping me inside.

"Have a seat." He pointed to the gurney.

I'd have rather stood, but I did as I was told. I sat at the edge of the hard cot, my lips tight and hands dug into the side of the bed.

He slammed the doors shut from the outside.

"Hey!" I screamed and jumped off the gurney, trying the door handle. He'd locked me inside. "Help!"

Everything outside the ambulance sounded muffled. Could they hear my cries for help?

"Help! Let me out!" My hands pounded hard against the metal doors.

A door slammed, and the engine of the ambulance purred to life. "Shit," I muttered. "Help! I'm locked in!" I tried again, but no one answered.

The ambulance jolted forward, and my feet fumbled until I gripped the nearby wall to steady myself. I had no phone, and Jaxson hadn't been in the best shape when I'd stupidly gone into the ambulance.

He wasn't a paramedic, but how had he fooled the others unless none of them were paramedics?

Hadn't Jaxson mentioned that the hospital was a two-hour drive?

I couldn't worry about Jaxson right now. I hoped Lincoln would find him.

I needed to escape.

The door would not open from the inside. I opened the nearest cabinet. Three shelves sat empty, but on the bottom shelf a small black duffel sat alone.

Bending down to reach for the duffel, I unzipped the bag to find a few supplies, nothing of any use to me: gauze, bandages, and medical tape. It held the same items that he'd used earlier for my forehead to appear as a paramedic without actually being one.

I hustled to the opposite side of the ambulance, checking the other cabinet. There were several vials, unlabeled but no syringes that I could see.

"Drugs?"

What were they doing with those? I smashed the vials against the floor. I would not chance that he'd try to use those on me.

The ambulance picked up speed as we traveled down the mountain, fleeing past the town.

While I couldn't see out any windows, with the heavy descent, the rush of the weight of the ambulance, I could hear the squeak of the brakes at every turn.

I slammed my fists against the thick partition between the driver and myself.

The driver ignored me. He sat alone in the front seat.

At least I only had one person to fight off when he eventually stopped and opened the door. He couldn't leave me in here forever.

"What do you want?" I shouted. My hands bunched together in fists as I pounded against the glass. "Let me go!"

The glass was dirty, thick, and had a goopy-dried coating around the edges. The window was made to open and slide, but someone had made sure that would not happen.

"Fuck!" Had he been involved in burning down my cabin? It seemed probable. "Who are you?"

Several vehicles sat in the middle of the mountain pass, blocking traffic.

"What the hell," he grumbled.

His voice, though muffled, I could hear, which meant he heard me just fine.

He slammed hard on the brakes, sending my body flinging through the back of the ambulance bay, smacking into the wall, the gurney slamming my knees.

I grimaced and swallowed back a groan from the pain. I didn't want him to get any ideas.

The tires squealed as he revved the engine.

A single-seat was positioned by the interior window, and I sat facing the front of the ambulance on my knees, clutching the seatback so that I could watch through the glass.

Several vehicles had blocked the main pass of the mountain. Had there been an accident?

Through the dirty opening, I spotted a familiar truck. My heart fluttered in my chest.

Could Jaxson be there?

No, I had to be delirious.

He was at the top of the mountain at home, lying unconscious on the snow outside of my burned-down cabin. More than one person owned that type of vehicle.

I could see figures outside their trucks, on the side of the road, but couldn't make out anyone's face. The glass was too dirty and distorted. Everyone appeared blurry.

"Help!" I screamed. Could anyone hear me?

He slammed the gas to the floor as the ambulance lurched forward, head on for the multitude of vehicles waiting below.

"Shit," I clutched the seat and reached for the buckle to spin around and secure the seatbelt, but it had been sliced in two. It was worthless.

The ambulance driver refused to slow down as the vehicle plowed down the mountain road, slamming into the trucks, SUVs, and police cruisers that had been sitting in the middle of the road.

I clung to the seat, the impact throwing me from the bench chair to the floor. "Help!" I shrieked.

Could the men outside hear me?

The crunch of metal drowned out their voices.

My head throbbed, and the ambulance's engine roared. The back of the vehicle fishtailed on what I could only surmise had been ice and snow.

The vehicle spun and catapulted down a ravine, throwing me around the back of the ambulance until darkness won over.

———————

Every part of me, inside and out, ached like fire dripping over my skin.

I groaned, and my eyelids fluttered open, the brightness forcing the pounding in my head to intensify and offering a warmth that made me imagine it was the sun.

"Looks like she's awake," a gruff voice echoed.

It took all my strength to focus, to stay awake and alert.

My fingers grazed the cold stone surface of where I curled up.

I wasn't in a bed.

There weren't any beeps of machines or sign that I'd been transported to a hospital. The last memory I had was of the accident, which meant that I hadn't escaped yet.

I exhaled a heavy breath and winced.

It hurt to breathe. That wasn't a good sign.

I rolled over on the hard floor and forced myself to sit, my back pressed up against a cold slab of cement.

The bright light that warmed me earlier had been the flicker of a single bulb in a darkened room.

Was I being held in someone's basement?

There was no sign of the ambulance or the forest floor.

The room smelled old, musty, and tickled my nose. I scrunched my face to keep from sneezing, glancing up at the dimly lit bulb.

Two men with long, thick beards sat on stools in the dark, knives in their hands, watching me.

I strummed my fingers over the cold stone floor. I was injured, but I could move. My fingers and toes wiggled. The men hadn't restrained me. There were no binds keeping me from moving.

"What do you want?" I asked, my voice hoarse, my mouth parched.

One man used his knife to whittle a stick, the end sharp.

Did he intend to use that on me?

I bit down on my tongue, the intense pain helping wake me from the foggy disconnect that surrounded my head. Had I not been in an accident, I would have surmised I had been drugged. Was it possible that both had happened?

The second man picked at the edge of his fingernails with his knife and then used it to clean between his teeth. With squinty eyes, he stood and towered from above. "Turns out there's a price on your head. We're just collecting the bounty. Sit tight."

That was the last thing I was prepared to do, sit and wait for my death.

What happened with Jaxson? Was he all right?

I didn't want these men to know that he meant anything to me, not if they'd use that against me too.

"How much am I worth?" If they were after money, I could convince them I had a bucket of wealth offshore. All they had to do was let me live.

Did they know who I was, what my ex-husband had been convicted of, or was this bounty because of my work with the agency?

The younger of the two men, the one whittling a long, sharp stick, pulled out his cell phone. "Buyer says she's worth the same dead or alive."

"Lucky for us," the second man said, his eyes lighting up with the prospect of my death.

"Whatever he's willing to give you, I can double it!" Would they see my bluff?

The man who stood above me tilted his head to the side and leaned down, knife in hand. The blade scratched my cheek. His putrid breath smelled of stale coffee.

"Yes, but I enjoy listening to the screams of a helpless woman when I stab her repeatedly. What fun is it for me if I let you live? This way, I get the money and my fun." He winked at me.

I leaned forward, coughing up bile.

His fingers yanked at my hair, pulling me to stand. He did nothing to help the throbbing sensation in my head except make it worse.

I clutched my forehead with one hand and the wall behind me with the other to keep from losing my balance. "Let me go." I would not be helpless.

I kicked him in the groin. He was swift, the blade of the knife pressed on my neck, my body tight against the cold cement wall.

"Are you sure you want to do that?" he asked, leaning in, his sick breath against my cheeks.

The hairs on my arms stood on end, and a chill ran down my spine.

I'd had plenty of practice fighting at the agency with a dummy knife, but under pressure, everything was different.

Fight or flight, and I froze.

CHAPTER TWENTY-TWO

JAXSON

Her faint scream brought me back and focused. I lifted my gloved hand, latching on to the mask around my face and yanking it off.

"You need to lie back down," the paramedic said as he hovered over me.

"The hell I do." I coughed as I pushed him away and stood, watching the ambulance tires spin on ice and snow before flying down the mountain road.

"You're not... where are you taking her?" I took several deep breaths, in through my nose and out through my mouth.

Already, I was doing better, more alert, less cloudy.

Whatever had been in that canister, it wasn't oxygen.
They'd tried to drug me.

Two firefighters were dousing the smoking remnants
of the cabin, keeping it from lighting ablaze again.
They were chatting amongst one another; I couldn't
hear them over the rush of water pounding the
rubble.

The paramedic had to know something. He must
have been involved. He didn't seem the least bit
stressed or surprised that his vehicle had just been
stolen with a woman in the back, screaming for help.

I landed a forceful blow to his face, wrestling him to
the ground, pinning him down and keeping his
hands far from his medical bag just a few feet away. I
didn't know what he had in there, whether it was a
gun or a sedative, but I would not let him touch me.

Another firefighter came up from behind the
paramedic with a spotlight. He turned on the light,
the brightness forcing the paramedic to shield his
eyes, blinding him as I kept him pinned to the snow.

"Get off me!" the paramedic shrieked. "You're crazy."

"You ain't seen crazy," I spat.

"What the hell is going on?" the firefighter asked. "You're not local EMS. You okay, sir?" He kept the spotlight on the paramedic, but his attention was now trained on me.

He tossed me a set of zip ties from his pocket. He recognized something was amiss as well.

There was only one ambulance in all of Breckenridge. The Adams family ran the EMS unit, and being a member of Eagle Tactical, I knew every one of the Adamses.

"I will be." I rolled the assailant around onto his stomach and tied his hands together before I stood. "What do you want with Ariella?" I yanked him around, making him sit in the cold, mushy snow.

"There's a bounty on her head. She's just a payday."

How many people were after her?

I pulled my phone from my pocket, dialed Lincoln and the rest of the Eagle Tactical team. I patched them through on a conference call together.

"Hey, what's going on, man?" Lincoln asked.

I'd left him at my house, just a few yards away, and he didn't know what had just transpired.

"Yeah, where are you?" Mason asked.

"Ariella's house burned down. We got caught up in the smoke and someone posing as a paramedic forced her into the back of the ambulance and took off with her down the mountain pass," I said. I further went into detail, demanding for them to call the local Breckenridge sheriff's office and block off the road.

"I'm on it," Declan answered.

"I also need a sheriff's unit brought up to the old cabin, the one Ariella purchased. One guy pretending to be a paramedic is in zip ties."

I didn't have cuffs handy, and while I could have easily dragged his ass down to the station, I needed to get to Ariella and protect her.

"You going to question him?" Lincoln asked.

I wanted to strap him down and interrogate him, shove the barrel of my gun against his bare skin.

That would take time, and it wasn't something I had a lot of right now.

"I'm leaving that up to the sheriff." There were too many witnesses with the fire department standing just a few feet away.

The type of interrogation I wanted to do would be off the books and highly illegal.

———

I rushed back between the tree line and over the bridge, skirting the house. The smoke had diminished. Lincoln approached the car. "I'm driving," he said.

I started the engine with my key fob and climbed into the passenger seat.

Lincoln didn't miss a beat, hurrying into the driver's side. The moment he shut the door, he had the vehicle in reverse and whisked us away from the house.

I yanked the seatbelt, securing it while Lincoln rushed us down the mountain pass, the road slick and wet from ice and snow. My stomach sank at the danger that lurked ahead.

"We'll get to her in time, don't worry." Lincoln's hands were tight on the steering wheel.

My foot tapped against the floor mats, anxiety creeping in, making the drive seem longer. "Were Izzie and Skylar okay?" I hadn't forgotten about them back at the house.

"They're fine. Izzie went down for a nap. Skylar was reading a book when I left her."

"Okay." I let out an anxious breath I hadn't realized that I'd been holding.

Lincoln flew down the mountain pass, a pro at taking the switchbacks in haste. He slowed as we drew near. A mess of vehicles were smashed and driven through, the ambulance already having left its wake.

"Look there!" Lincoln pointed at the tire tracks off the road and the ambulance down at the bottom of the ravine on its side. He pulled off the road and hit the brakes.

I threw open the truck door and hurried down the ravine, my boots skidding down the side of the mountain along with me. I didn't care if I landed on my ass, as long as I found her.

Mason and Aiden were already down by the ambulance with the sheriff and several other townsfolk conversing.

"Ariella!"

Mason spotted me first and shook his head no.

My stomach sank.

I didn't know if that meant she wasn't there, or if worse, she didn't make it. I refused to accept that she'd died. There wasn't a body as far as I could see. Unless she was in the back of the ambulance?

"Where is she?" I shouted, sliding down, my feet slipping under me, but I caught my balance. My arms out, I steadied myself before running the last leg of distance toward my buddies.

"She's not here," Mason said, his eyes filled with sorrow. He didn't want to be the one to convey bad news, but someone had to tell me what happened.

That wasn't enough of an answer for me. I needed more. "Where is she?"

Lincoln came up from behind, having followed me down the slope of the ravine. He poked his head into the ambulance bay, examining the scene and any evidence left behind.   .

I exhaled a loud breath, my heart hammering in my chest. "Any leads?" I wouldn't abandon Ariella. She needed me more than ever.

"Declan is back at Eagle Tactical, running surveillance and scouring the dark web for leads. Although he pulled down the bounty earlier from the net, it's clear someone saw it and acted on it while the information was still fresh," Mason said.

Lincoln shoved his hands into his coat pocket. "There's not much to go on other than the ambulance was definitely not used for medical purposes. The equipment is pretty scarce in there, which means there likely wasn't anything she could have used as a weapon, either."

"She's smart." She worked for the C.I.A. at one point, and I trusted that she'd do everything in her power to stay alive.

She just needed to survive long enough until we found her.

Shoving my fingers into my coat, I kept my head down, examining broken branches and a single set of footprints that appeared to be a size 12 men's that were farther from the group.

I followed the trail, not sure what to expect. "Look, there's one set of prints."

The footprints sunk into the ground, potential evidence that she'd been carried and unable to walk. There didn't appear to be a second set of prints coming back, either, which meant it couldn't have been the sheriff or anyone else helping with the search party.

"The mountain pass runs just south of here. They could have gone down the road to another pickup point. There's no way they planned on keeping the ambulance and not being seen," Mason said.

"Maybe, but south is that direction." I pointed south and then continued to follow the footprints that led west. "They didn't go to the road. It's possible they got turned around."

If we were lucky, they were still in the forest. I held up my hand, signaling to wait.

Crouching down, I examined droplets of fresh blood on the snow. "She was here." I'd never been more certain in my life.

I hurried, following the trail of footprints and droplets of blood that were mixed and mottled, difficult to find with branches strewn everywhere.

Lincoln, Mason, and Aiden followed at my heel as we scoured the forest, making sure we weren't being played and the tracks had been a diversion. That didn't appear to be the case.

I wanted to scream out for her, but if we were close along with the assailant, I didn't want to further put her life in danger.

In the distance, a cabin sat nestled in the woods, four black SUVs in the driveway. "Any chance you guys brought a gun?" I didn't want to go in outnumbered and unarmed.

"Did we come armed?" Lincoln laughed under his breath.

He lifted his shirt, showing me his gun. He then reached for his ankle holster, retrieving his spare weapon and handing it to me. "Looks like I'm saving your ass again, Monroe."

"Just like old times," I joked, "where you think you're saving me, but in actuality, I'm rescuing you."

With his gun drawn, he moved behind a tree as we grew closer. "Keep thinking that," Lincoln said.

Aiden crouched down, pulling a switchblade from his pocket. "I'll slash their tires and keep them from getting away."

"Good thinking." We didn't want them taking Ariella off the property. I gestured for us to fan out. We needed to surround the cabin, find out what awaited us inside.

The car door of the SUV slammed shut. I snuck behind a tree, doing my best to camouflage. When I woke up this morning, I hadn't thought this was how my day would go. I bet Ariella didn't think the same, either.

Slow and even breaths. The cold sucked the air out of my lungs and burned, but I ignored the pain in my chest.

Our footprints were fresh, but that didn't worry me as much as the sound of branches cracking under our boots. My foot came down slow and cautious as I moved from one tree with my sight on another to use as a minimal form of protection.

Aiden needed to be careful with the men outside by the SUV.

I held my breath.

He stabbed one tire before moving around the vehicle to hit another.

The men stood outside and talked, oblivious to what happened around them. That was good. It meant they were distracted.

We just needed to keep them that way while we found and rescued Ariella.

I took another step closer, coming up to the cabin. I crouched beside the window and peered in, careful not to be seen. There were gruff voices, but no one in the room faced the window.

A loud, feminine, ear-piercing scream echoed through the house.

I didn't wait any longer; I rushed toward the nearest entrance and barreled in through the back door, gun drawn with Lincoln and Mason right behind me.

They had heard her cry for help too.

CHAPTER TWENTY-THREE

ARIELLA

Fear drenched me to the core of my existence.

I trembled under the blade of his knife. The smirking bastard with breath old and putrid nicked my neck, reminding me he was in charge.

I could do this.

I had to do this. I talked myself up, my hands in fists at my sides, gathering strength.

I stomped on his toes, his boots thin, then shoved my knee hard up into his groin.

He doubled over in pain to grab his family jewels when the knife clanked to the floor. I yanked my knee hard up again, this time into his face, before ramming him headfirst into the wall.

He fell like a ton of bricks.

I bent down and snatched his knife. The handle trembled in my hands. It was my only line of defense to get out of the cellar.

"Nice one. You know if you kill him, it means more money for me," said the second man who had sat on his stool whittling his stick. He stood, the sharp instrument in his grip.

I stepped over the imbecile, keeping my back to the wall for protection.

There were no windows in the basement. The small space closed in on me like a coffin.

My fingers grazed the cement, reminding me it wasn't moving. The dizziness was all in my head.

The room was constrictive, and as car doors slammed, beads of sweat trickled down my forehead.

"Let me go," I said with as much conviction as I could muster. "I told you I have money. I can give you far more than anyone else will for killing me."

I'd tell a million lies if it would save my life. Would he fall for it?

"Unlike Carter, I don't want to kill you. I prefer to play with the merchandise." He snickered and unfastened his belt.

My eyes widened, and my stomach somersaulted. I gripped the handle of the knife until my knuckles turned white.

"Come here, girly," he said, stalking toward me.

I screamed loud and hard. My lungs burned from the pain. My throat would be hoarse tomorrow, but I didn't care if it meant that I lived to see another sunrise.

I screamed again, hoping to bring the men from outside down to the cellar. They wanted me dead, and while I didn't want to end up six feet under, I also wasn't about to get raped by a madman after a payday.

I skirted the wall, my gaze finding nothing, the only weapon in my defense a blade that was smaller and meant getting closer than his sharpened stick.

"We could play a game," he whispered. He was grabbing my arm and pinning it back above my head, forcing the damned weapon to fall. At least he didn't have his shaft.

It took all the courage I had to muster the words he wanted to hear. Could I convince him to let me go? "I like games," I said and swallowed the lump that formed in my throat.

His decrepit hand stroked my cheek, and I turned my head away, refusing to look at him. He grabbed me by the chin and forced my face to look at him. "Doesn't look like you enjoy this game very much," he said.

He leaned closer to me, his body just inches from mine.

The room spun.

Had the thermostat been suddenly turned up? Sweat licked my skin and my stomach recoiled.

I stomped his foot, but he wore steel-toed boots, offering him protection and only making the bottoms of my feet throb.

I winced but didn't let him see my discomfort or surprise that the maneuver hadn't worked.

His hand that had been on my chin fell to my knee. "Don't even think about fighting this, girly. You know you want it." He leaned toward me.

"I could never want anyone like you!" I spat in his face and squirmed to escape his grasp.

The knife lay on the floor out of my reach with my hands pinned above my head.

He kept me trapped, and though I attempted to use the force of my entire body to fight him, he was taller than I was, heftier, and had me restrained.

"I do like a girl who fights," he said and snickered.

The other man who had attacked me earlier and had been lying on the ground stirred awake.

He grabbed my legs, keeping me from kicking either of them again.

I screamed again, and the bastard who had me pinned to the wall and my hands clamped above my head shoved his hand over my mouth.

I bit down on his fingers, unwilling to give in to his demands or temptations.

"You bitch!" he snarled and threw his hand back, smacking me hard across the face. "I'll show you," he said, unzipping his pants.

Heavy footsteps pounded against the ceiling of the cellar. "Help!" I screamed, thrashing as I tried to break free of both men.

"Ariella!" Jaxson's voice was music to my ears, the sweetest symphony I'd ever heard in my life.

His boots slammed against the stairs. He and his buddies came tearing down the basement to help.

"What the hell?" The man spun around, pants at his ankles.

The other man on the floor released his grasp from my legs and grabbed the switchblade to defend himself.

"I'll kill you!" Jaxson screamed, slamming his fist into the first man's face, the guy with bloody fingers. I hadn't realized how deep I'd bitten down. Seeing the blood made me gag.

Lincoln and Mason tore down the dimly lit stairs with Jaxson, disarming both men, knocking them momentarily unconscious.

I threw myself into Jaxson's embrace.

Lincoln pulled out a pair of zip ties and secured both attacker's hands to ensure they were no longer a threat.

Being wrapped in Jaxson's strong, warm arms made me relax. I rubbed my cheek against his chest and closed my eyes, drinking in his strength.

Lincoln cleared his throat. "Sorry to break up the reunion, but there's still a bunch of guys out front with Aiden. We need to get out of here, now."

Lincoln headed up the stairwell first, gun drawn.

"Stay behind me," Jaxson said, leading me up the stairs. Like his shadow, I clung to him.

The men gave one another signals. He nodded for me to follow.

Each step they took was silent, absent as if they never were here.

Shouts from the basement erupted. The two men downstairs had woken up.

"We need to move, now!" Jaxson grabbed my arm and pulled me to run with him as he led me out the back door and into the forest.

"Where's your truck?" I'd heard a car door earlier, not long before Jaxson had come down and rescued me.

We kept running through the forest with no end in sight. I glanced over my shoulder. Men in black suits with guns were trailing behind us.

"Way too far." His hand clutched mine, a lifeline.

He pulled me through the forest.

I wasn't out of shape. Ordinarily, I could have run miles without a hitch, but I'd been assaulted twice today and survived an accident in an ambulance.

It wasn't my best day.

He pulled me tight against a tree, his body pressed against mine, protecting me.

Bullets whizzed by our heads. I froze, frightened. The sound of a gunshot rippled through my body, forcing the adrenaline to rear its ugly head.

I trembled but found solace in the warmth of Jaxson's body pressing me tight against the rough bark.

His embrace was firm, protective, and warm. His touch was strong while his attention was entirely on keeping me safe.

Lincoln found a tree for cover.

Mason did the same.

"We can't keep running," Jaxson said. He wasn't talking to me.

Lincoln, Mason, and Jaxson began firing their weapons at the men in suits with guns.

"Who are they?" They didn't look like the C.I.A.. They weren't the same grungy bastard types who had attacked me at the resort or burned down my cabin and abducted me for money.

"Bounty hunters," Jaxson said.

My hands pulled him closer, willing him to do whatever he needed to do to save me. He wasn't joking.

These were men on a mission to kill.

"Since when do bounty hunters wear suits?" I tried to make a joke. Probably bad timing as he pressed himself entirely against me, his face in mine, taking cover as bullets rained around us.

His forehead leaned against mine. My fingers tugged at his jacket. I shivered, the coat he loaned me long since discarded.

"You're freezing, shit." Jaxson tried making himself as small as possible, not to let his limbs extend from beyond the cover of the tree trunk.

He slipped off his coat and put it around my shoulders. "You need this more than I do." His eyes twinkled with that charm that only Jaxson had.

He was a hero in every sense of the word.

"You're going to be cold," I said, attempting to reason with him why I shouldn't take his spare coat since I'd already taken possession of his last jacket, and that hadn't ended well for his clothes.

Lincoln and Mason fired off shots at the men. The sound of gunfire coming at us seemed to diminish. Were the men dead, injured, or out of bullets?

"I'll be fine," he scoffed. "Now, stay here. Don't move." Jaxson raised his gun again, firing off several more shots before silence ensued.

Was it over?

I trembled against the trunk of the tree, warmer as I slid my arms into his coat but unable to move, too afraid the men played dead.

What if they were waiting for us to move, to sneak out from hiding and shoot me?

"All clear!" Aiden shouted from where the bullets had been flying from earlier.

"Don't move," Jaxson said.

Wordlessly, I nodded. I could handle not moving. I was good at that, especially right now when my body wasn't cooperating. Even if I wanted to walk, I didn't think myself capable.

The trunk of the tree held me up. My weight pressed tight. I let my fingers graze over the wood, memorizing every detail, the texture against the pads of my fingertips—anything to take my mind off what had just transpired.

Jaxson poked his head out, his hands on my hips as Mason, Lincoln, and Aiden tracked through the forest back toward the cabin from where the gunshots had gone off.

"All clear," Mason said.

Jaxson didn't so much as release his hold or move away like I thought he might. He held me, kept me protected. Was he worried it wasn't over? Did he think I couldn't look after myself?

His jaw was tight, square, and clenched. "We left those two goons tied up. It probably won't be long until they want their revenge. Boys like that don't appreciate losing."

"Great," I muttered under my breath.

"They got their revenge and then some. They need a body bag," Aiden said, pointing at both men lying in a pool of their own blood on the snow-covered ground.

I shivered.

"It's over," Jaxson said. His shoulders relaxed. The tension slipped out of him.

The warmth of the sun began to fade as it set. I wasn't quite at ease. "Is it?" I whispered.

The men from the resort, the thugs who attacked me earlier in the day, were expecting four million dollars, and I didn't have a cent.

———

Jaxson held me tight. His hand latched around mine. We waited outside the front of the cabin, the one where I'd been dragged and nearly raped, for the police to arrive.

I wasn't looking forward to giving my statement. I didn't want to relive the trauma over again.

All I wanted was to go home and soak in a warm bath.

Except I didn't have a bath anymore. Hell, I didn't have a house anymore.

The police finally came along, taking their sweet time. The Eagle Tactical guys had to answer questions of their own about the incident, as did I.

I didn't like being separated from them, especially Jaxson, but we were outside and only a few yards away. I could see him, but not being safe in his warm arms made it difficult.

Just as the last statements were given, Declan strolled up in his truck offering us a ride.

I climbed into the backseat sandwiched between Jaxson and Lincoln.

Aiden grabbed the front seat.

Mason cleared his throat.

"Sorry, man, there's no room," Lincoln joked with Mason.

"Looks like Mason's going to sit on Jaxson's lap," Aiden grinned.

Jaxson rolled his eyes.

"You're groaning because you know it's true," Aiden said.

Jaxson's gaze met mine. "You're going to have to sit on my lap for the ride back to Eagle Tactical."

"Okay," I answered a little too quickly. They didn't notice. Jaxson didn't budge from his position on the side, and I scooted onto his lap.

Lincoln scooted over, making room for Mason. He jogged around the back of the truck, and Declan started to take off, the door open, messing with him.

"Don't be an ass!" Mason chased after the truck before Declan softly came to a stroll, making Mason climb in while the vehicle was still moving. Albeit it wasn't moving fast, I couldn't hide the grin on my face. He deserved it, just a little.

Mason flung himself into the truck and slammed the door.

"Got everyone?" Declan glanced in the rearview mirror, taking a brief mental headcount before hitting the gas and hightailing it out of there.

The backseat was a little too cozy. I shifted on Jaxson's lap, my cheeks burning from the heat or his proximity.

All the men of Eagle Tactical were eye candy. To be thrust in the backseat on Jaxson's lap and practically sandwiched in with Lincoln, wasn't so bad. Mason was growing on me too. He saved my life, even after I'd been an ass to him. Whether it was well-deserved was still debatable.

"Thanks, you guys," I whispered, my hands trembling.

Jaxson's warm, strong embrace wrapped around my waist, his fingers against my hips. Every part of me burned like I was on fire, but my heart ached, conflicted with doubt. He'd left after we'd been intimate without so much as a word goodbye. How could I forgive that transgression?

Should I forgive him?

He saved my life. I owed him my life, but did I owe him my heart?

"All in a day's work," Mason said. He gave me a faint smile. Did he no longer hate me? That had to be good news, especially if I saw Jaxson again.

Conflicted was the understatement of the century. Everything about Jaxson was perfect, but I was a mess. He deserved better, someone who made him happy.

He had a daughter, and then there was Emma.

The guys laughed and joked on the rest of the ride back to Eagle Tactical. I sat quietly, lost in my thoughts and the heat of the moment between Jaxson and myself. His lap was warm, comfortable, his embrace even more magical.

I whimpered, disappointed when we arrived, and I needed to climb out of the truck. I had thought no one heard me, but Jaxson raised an inquisitive eyebrow.

I shut my lips fast and glanced away, humiliated.

The guys all piled out of the truck.

"I need a ride to my vehicle," Lincoln said.

"Ariella and I need a ride back to my house," Jaxson said, already deciding that I was going with him.

I wasn't sure where I was going or what would happen next. I didn't have a house. Everything had burned in the disaster. I still had a date with thugs who wanted four million dollars that I'd missed and a cell phone that had been smashed in the fight at the resort.

My life was a mess.

"Lincoln, I'll give you a ride if you're buying me dinner," Aiden joked.

"Fine. Never a dull moment or a day off," Lincoln said.

Declan hurried over toward Jaxson and me. He shoved his hand into his coat pocket, retrieving a smartphone. "A small present. You can thank Jaxson later," Declan said with a wink. He handed me the phone. My mouth practically hit the floor.

"What are you—I don't understand," I said. My fingers grazed over the crystal screen. It appeared brand new. There were no scratches or scuffs, pristine condition. It was better than my flip phone.

"When you mentioned your cell phone had been destroyed earlier, I texted and asked him to set you up with a new phone. He also made sure that no one else can trace your whereabouts. Other than us," Jaxson said. He laughed.

I wasn't sure if he was joking or not. I didn't care. "Thank you," I said to both men. They'd saved my life. If they wanted to implant a tracker on me or put one in my phone, I was at their mercy. I owed them.

Declan gestured at the phone in my hand. "We tied it to your recent phone plan. It's already active, and anyone who needs to get ahold of you will be able to."

Mason hurried over to us. "Do you still need a ride home?"

Jaxson pulled me tighter against him. The wind outside whipped through the air, stinging my cheeks, but his proximity warmed me. "Yes, we both could use a ride back to my place."

I shuffled my feet and shoved my hands into my coat pockets. Jaxson's scent surrounded me, especially on his coat. He had to be freezing, but he hid it rather well. Did he always pretend to be the tough guy?

"Follow me," Mason said, hurrying to his truck.

Jaxson grabbed my arm, linking ours together as he walked me to Mason's truck and opened the back door for me.

I slid into the backseat, the leather chilly against my bottom, forcing an unwanted shiver. I had no home to return to, but if Jaxson insisted I go back with him, I would not say no.

I didn't want to be alone. Not until I knew I wasn't in any further danger.

Jaxson shut the door for me and climbed into the front seat. Mason started the truck and pulled out of the lot.

"Drop off Ariella at my house, then I want to make a stop, just you and me," Jaxson said.

Where did they plan to go after dropping me off? I relaxed in the backseat, staring out the window as we headed up the mountain pass. I pulled the new phone from my pocket, my finger scrolling through the contents he'd been able to retrieve off the cloud, including my contacts.

I had several missed calls and a few text messages from Emma asking me where I was and if everything was okay. I'd call her back tonight when I had a few minutes alone.

I checked my voice messages, my stomach in knots when I heard my boss, Bridget Sanders from the Blue Sky Resort, fire me. "Shit."

"What's that?" Mason asked. He glanced at me in the rearview mirror.

My cheeks burned. Jaxson wasn't happy when I'd cursed in front of Izzie. It was a nasty habit I had trouble breaking.

"I just got fired from my job." I deleted the message and shut off the screen for my phone, pushing the button on the side to put it into silent mode. I didn't want to hear from anyone else. My mood turned sour.

"I can't believe they fired you," Jaxson said.

Mason's gaze met mine again, his focus back on the road a moment later. "Wait. They likely don't know what happened, that you were kidnapped and unable to get to work. You can't fault them for being in the dark. I'm sure if you talk with your boss, you can have your old job back."

I didn't even care about that stupid place or the job. The money was crap pay, but it was employment. "Doubtful. They fired me because, according to them, I lied on my resume since I didn't disclose my married name or my previous employer." I ran my fingers through my unkempt hair, tugging at the strands with a groan. "In her words, I'm too much of a liability."

Mason and Jaxson exchanged a silent glance.

"It never ends," I seethed. My fingers dug into the leather seat. As if that was the worst of my problems. "Those men will be looking for their money." I'd never made the drop at sundown.

Jaxson shifted in the passenger seat and turned around to face me. "You're under our protection. We plan on making that clear."

CHAPTER TWENTY-FOUR

JAXSON

My blood boiled from hearing that Ariella had been fired from the resort.

She was too good for them, overqualified to be cleaning toilets and changing bed sheets.

"I'm under your protection?" Ariella's soft whisper caught in her throat. I almost couldn't hear her, but I strained to listen to every word.

"Of course." Didn't she realize how much she meant to me already? I cared deeply for a woman who held a closet of secrets. Would she ever let me inside?

Declan had texted Lincoln and me the information he'd pulled from the resort. The surveillance he acquired had taken no time to identify the two men who had attacked Ariella at the resort.

They were commonly referred to as 'off-gridders' living on the outskirts of town together in a commune.

I knew a few of them through my work with Eagle Tactical. They were usually harmless, feared authority, and were reclusive individuals who avoided anyone who wasn't one of them.

In the simplest of terms, they were shady.

Why had they gone after Ariella?

Had they been victims in the Ponzi scheme as well?

We still didn't have all the answers, and while it looked like her ex-husband may not have been rightfully convicted, the evidence still pointed to him.

Had the C.I.A. set him up? Had they intended to set up Ariella as well, and she'd got away with a decent lawyer?

Mason turned down the road for my house. "I'm going to walk her inside," I said. Mason left the engine running as I hopped out from the truck the moment he pulled to a standstill.

I opened the back door of the truck for Ariella and offered her my hand. Her eyes fell on the snow and slush as she climbed out of the truck.

I held her close and could smell the smoke from the fire on her clothes and skin. It tickled my nose. I probably needed a shower too.

"Come on inside." I ushered her to my front door, unlocked the deadbolt, disarmed the alarm, and led her inside.

She slipped off her winter boots first and then my jacket, handing it to me. "Thank you for this," she said.

The energy I'd harbored had me forgetting how cold it had been outside, how my fingers were numb. I slipped on the coat, smelling a mix of her womanly scent and smoke mingled together.

Skylar hurried down the stairs and stopped midway, her hand hovering on the railing. "Is everything okay?"

"Yes. Thank you for keeping an eye on Izzie. Ariella will be staying with us." I didn't elaborate for how long. It wasn't something we'd discussed, but the obvious fact her house was a pile of ash showed it wouldn't be a few short days. "Can you show her to my bedroom for a fresh change of clothes? She may want to shower and get cleaned up. I'm sure you're familiar with where the linens are located."

Skylar had stayed over enough times that she knew her way around my house.

"I'll show her around," Skylar said.

"Thank you," Ariella said. With quiet steps, she approached the bottom stair and turned around, glancing over her shoulder at me. "I'll be here when you get back."

"I expect nothing less. I'll set the alarm. Don't open the door for anyone, is that understood?"

"Yes," they both said in unison.

I wanted to pull Ariella into my arms, kiss the pain away, the worry and doubt she had etched to her face. Instead, I armed the alarm and rushed out the front door, locking it with my key.

Mason sat in the truck, his fingers strumming the steering wheel. The bone-tingling chill licked my spine. I shivered and jogged to the truck.

"Ready to kick some ass?"

"Let's hope it doesn't come to that."

Mason reversed our course and headed back to the mountain pass.

We headed another mile north, and then we took a sharp left on a snow-covered trail, a bit too narrow for the truck.

Thin branches walloped the truck while we drove through the thicket of trees. Mason didn't seem the least bit annoyed by it. Had it been my truck, I'd have preferred a walk in the cold over scratching the paint on the exterior.

Mason shot me a look as we climbed out. It was just the two of us. We didn't come for a fight; we came with a warning.

With my hand on my holster and Mason at my side, we walked along the snow-covered stone driveway.

My boots crunched the snow, the slush packed down from multiple vehicles that drove over the area.

The commune housed more families than I probably was aware of. I knew of at least six who lived in the complex, but there were far more whom I didn't know.

The outside structure was made of wood, and from first glance, the building appeared large and stylish, a lodge in the middle of the forest. It had probably been built for a wealthy family several generations ago. It had been stripped down to its bare essentials, which didn't include running water, heat, or electricity.

Ariella had thought her cabin was sparse.

While the off-gridders had a large plot of land and shelter over their heads, there wasn't much inside. It was as basic as it could be.

I'd been inside occasionally and hoped today wasn't one of the times. The interior always smelled musty and foul, like tent city in the summer, wreaking of urine.

By the front entrance, which was always wide open, the door abandoned, probably destroyed and never replaced, stood a guard with a shotgun.

"It's Jayden," I said, keeping my voice down.

"How do you want to play this?" Mason asked, glancing at me out of the corner of his eye.

"Tight, but cautious. He's not the same man he was back in the old days."

We'd served in the military with Jayden. He'd been a buddy of ours, but somewhere along the way after the war, we'd lost contact. He had guarded the compound. I always thought he'd be on the right side of the law, but he refused an invitation to come work with us at Eagle Tactical.

We never understood why.

I approached Jayden first with Mason right at my hip, defending me.

Jayden didn't budge from his position at the door, standing guard. "What brings the Eagle Tactical guys out here today?" His eyes raked over me, landing on my holster. "You came armed?"

"Don't I always?" I didn't go anywhere without packing heat. "We're here to speak to Ian Connor and Seth Rogers."

One glance at the surveillance footage sent to my phone, and I knew these men. They were scumbags, but they weren't blackmailers or extortionists. The fact they roughed up a girl, Ariella, wasn't their typical M.O..

Jayden shifted his weight on his feet. I took that as a sign of discomfort, although his face appeared blank and emotionless. "What about?"

"Your guys threatened and assaulted one of mine," I seethed between clenched teeth. Stepping closer, one hand balled into a fist, with the other I pulled my weapon and shoved it into Jayden's face.

"You'll let me inside." I was tired of his childish games and antics.

Mason cleared his throat and rested a hand on my arm. "Jaxson." His tone warned me to cool off or calm down.

We weren't going in for a firefight, but I damn well would bring them one if they so much as looked at Ariella again.

"Is this official Eagle Tactical business?" Jayden asked.

I lowered my gun, shoved my shoulder into Jayden's chest, and knocked him backward and into the doorjamb.

I didn't wait for an invitation. I plowed through the front entrance. "Ian Connor! Seth Rogers!" I shouted, letting the bastards know I had come for them.

Mason was at my side. "You sure you want to do that?" he whispered.

I wouldn't let anything happen to *my* girl. We would be quick, in and out, and then we could go home and call it a night. I'd throw myself in the shower, let the scalding water rush down my body, and wipe away my sins—every one of them.

Ian strolled around the corner, his hands shoved into his jeans, shoulders slumped. "What brings you boys to my neck of the woods?" he asked. He edged closer, just out of my reach, taking his sweet ass time.

My eyes narrowed like a hawk, my focus solely on Ian. "The fact you haven't learned how to treat a lady with respect," I said.

I shoved my gun into its holster on my hip and grabbed him by the shoulders, his t-shirt, thin and threadbare, torn. Forcing his knees to the ground, I shoved my leg hard upwards. My knee caught his chin as I barreled into him. As I pinned him to the floor, he wrestled to get away from me.

"Get off me!" Ian scurried to escape my clutches.

"What? Don't enjoy being manhandled? You should keep your filthy paws off my girl," I growled at him. He kicked me, sweeping his feet out to knock me on my ass. "Bastard."

"Me? You come to my home," he said, gasping for breath, "and attack me!"

I ignored the throes of people standing around watching us in the center fighting like wild animals.

He deserved a good ass-kicking for what he did to Ariella. I wanted him to remember the pain.

"You need a hand?" Mason asked. He folded his arms across his chest and towered above.

He seemed to enjoy the show. "Just keep an eye out for the other asshole," I muttered.

"Already watching him," Mason said. His eyes were on him, and I glanced across the large room and laid eyes on Seth. Mason stalked across the room, and I didn't have to watch to know he'd take care of him in the same way I was looking after Ian.

I pulled back my fist, landing a blow to Ian's face, stunning him momentarily. Standing up, I would not lie around when a man's ass needed kicking.

"What girl would ever want the likes of you?" Ian asked, getting to his feet. He lunged for me, headfirst into my stomach, knocking me backward. I tripped over someone who stuck out their foot, giving Ian a hand.

"Fucking bastards," I growled and planted my hands on the floor to stand when I realized my hip was ice cold, my gun gone.

I glanced over my shoulder to find the barrel of my weapon staring back at me, in the hands of Emma

Foster, my daughter's biological mother. The same woman I told to leave town.

What the fuck was she doing here?

"Get up." Emma held my weapon. Her hands trembled as she pointed it at me.

Slowly and cautiously, I stood, careful not to make any sudden movements. "Give me the gun." I held out my hand, waiting for her to relinquish control over the weapon.

The brunette with brown eyes who had charmed me once would not do it ever again.

"No." She refused to lower the barrel of my gun.

So be it. I would not stand there and wait for her to shoot me, accident or otherwise. On second thought, it might not be an accident if she had returned to Breckenridge to get Izzie back.

"Last chance, Emma, or I'm about to break your finger." No one said I didn't warn her.

She huffed under her breath. "I have the gun, Jaxson," she said, reminding me she thought she was in power.

I had military and survival training. With a sloth grip, four fingers, and not using my thumb, I slammed my right hand against her wrist. With my left hand, I spun the gun from her palm and turned it toward her.

"Motherfucker!" she screamed, her thumb on the trigger forcing her digit to break.

"I warned you."

Behind me, Jayden's overpowering presence resonated, his footfalls not the least bit silent. "Back off!" I shouted.

Jayden held up his hands. "Just checking on the girl." He wrapped an arm around her shoulders, walking her away from the crowd to take care of her.

Anger soared within me. What was Emma doing at the commune? Did she live here now?

"You know Emma?" Ian asked, a smile on his face, laughing under his breath and wincing after getting the shit kicked out of him. "Of course, you do. We all do. The girl gives magnificent head."

I rammed into him headfirst, tossing him to the ground, scuffling on the floor. My fists slammed against his chest, one punch after another.

I wasn't happy with Emma, but I liked even less the way Ian spoke about her. "You will learn to respect women."

"I respect them. I respect letting them ride me," he said and sneered.

Ian knew just what to say to get under my skin. He slammed his forehead upward against mine, knocking me back for a moment and landing a blow to my left cheek.

I hadn't expected him to make a good play.

Fuck, that hurt.

Snickering, he pushed me off him.

I stumbled backward. My head throbbed, and while I was prepared to kick his scrawny ass until he bled to death, that wasn't why we came.

We were here with a warning and a firm message that she was under our protection. "Ariella is off-limits. You and your buddies stay away, or you're going to deal with Eagle Tactical." I made my voice loud and clear for all the off-gridders in the complex to know that if they messed with her, they messed with all of us.

"Fine, keep your tight little Ariella. We've got Emma for a good time," Ian said and winked. He was trying to get a rise out of me.

I threw another punch and landed on his chest. I slammed my knee upwards into his groin and watched him double over, collapsing onto the ground. I stared down, waiting for him to get up.

He groaned and cried like a little baby. He was definitely alive, just discovering the burn of a good ass-kicking.

Mason had Seth in a headlock, the off-gridder on his knees. "How'd you find out who Ariella was?"

Seth's hands flailed and Mason loosened his grip to let him answer.

He coughed and gasped for air, bent forward, his hands on his knees. "At Lumberjack Shack, Ian and I overheard two guys talking about her, how she was loaded. Emma mentioned getting drinks with her friend Ariella. We put two and two together. How many Ariellas could there possibly be in Breckenridge? A google search turned up the rest of the information. We thought it'd be an easy payday and a fresh start for all of us."

Mason slowly eased up and let go, tossing the thug on the ground.

I took the opportunity to step forward and crouched down, fisting his shirt in my hand, snarling at him. I ignored his stench, the smell of piss and filth that burned my nostrils. "Ariella is under our protection. You so much as look at her the wrong way and you'll find yourself in an unmarked grave."

"You've been warned," Mason said, standing beside me. "Next time we won't be so nice." He patted me on the back, a silent message that we were done and to let the asshole go.

The crowd dispersed, no longer interested if a fight wasn't ensuing. I didn't see Emma. Jayden probably was tending to her wounds.

With our message made loud and clear, we left the compound and headed for the truck.

"Listen," I said, climbing into the vehicle. "With what happened tonight, the fact Emma was at the compound, do me a favor, and let's not say anything to Ariella. The two of them are friends, and I don't want to further complicate matters."

Ariella was delicate, and while she'd been through hell, I didn't want her questioning Emma's motives for being her friend. That would be my job to deal with, not hers.

Mason started the engine and stomped on the gas. "It's not like I have coffee with her every morning. Speaking of which, I'm surprised you didn't bring up that we could use someone like her on our team, ex-C.I.A., surveillance skills, and she needs a job."

"It had crossed my mind." I wasn't sure the guys would go for it. We were always looking for talent and people we could trust.

"I'll talk to the others, but I think we could make it work under one condition."

There it was, the catch that made my stomach sink. "Which is?"

Deep down, I already knew the answer. We were equal owners, the guys and I, in Eagle Tactical. She would be our employee.

"You two have to keep it professional. If she works for us, then you're her boss. You can't sleep with her and not expect matters to get more complicated than they already are at the moment," Mason said.

My jaw tightened. I didn't like his stupid rules, but he was sensible. I needed to think about the team and Ariella, what was best for them, not myself. "Just friends."

Could I let her go because it was in her best interest? The thought tore me up inside. But a relationship was far more dangerous. She would be in the office, I would be in the field, and we couldn't let our feelings impede our missions.

Mistakes can cost lives.

Distractions were deadly.

"Right." Mason shot me a look as we turned down the road for my house. "Can you keep in it your pants while the two of you are living together?"

CHAPTER TWENTY-FIVE

ARIELLA

Every inch of the house smelled of Jaxson, musky and intense. It tickled my nose.

The giant glass windows overlooked the forest, and as night fell, there wasn't much to see.

Could anyone who traveled up the mountain see us?

Jaxson hadn't warned me to close the curtains or shut off the lights. He'd set the alarm for the house. We would be safe. I had to believe that, or I would never be able to settle down.

"Come on," Skylar said, stomping up the stairs.

"Daddy?" Izzie came around the corner. Her eyes lit up when they landed on me. She squealed and jumped, her eyes wide and cheeks rosy. As she threw her arms in the air for me to hold her, I bent down, hugging her to my chest.

"Your daddy will be home soon," I said. She squeezed me tight, my body melting under her innocence.

Her world was protected because of Jaxson. She had no idea the dangers of evil and what horrors men were capable of.

"Play with me?" Her hand latched tight onto mine, dragging me toward her room. I needed to shower, get dressed, and clean up, but I couldn't say no to her.

Skylar stepped between us, breaking Izzie's hold on my hand. "Isabella, I'm sure Ariel has better things to do with her time."

"Are you the Little Mermaid?" Izzie began jumping up and down, clapping her hands together. "Can you sing? Do you have a tail?"

Great. Now I had to disappoint a toddler. My singing voice was atrocious, and I definitely did not have a mermaid's tail, or any tail, for that matter. "I don't sing as beautifully as Ariel," I said. I turned to Skylar. "My name is Ariella."

"Sure, whatever." She shrugged and shot me a look. "That's what I said."

"It's not." I pinched the bridge of my nose, too exhausted to argue. Dropping my hand, I folded my arms across my chest.

What was her problem?

The glint in Izzie's eyes was enough to settle my nerves and soothe my boiling blood. I bent down to Isabella's level, making eye contact with her. "I would love to see your room."

Izzie snatched my hand and dragged me down the hall. She rushed inside her bedroom and stood waiting for me to join her.

I flipped on the light and was met with an abundance of mermaids all over her bedroom. I covered my mouth with my hand to keep the giddy grin from my lips and tried not to burst out laughing.

The girl was obsessed with mermaids.

The walls were painted cerulean with white and pink foam bubbles. Near the window, a mermaid's tail sparkled and shined, with glittery hues of teal and a thin silver outline. "Did your dad paint your bedroom?"

Impressive would have been an understatement. Someone with a lot of artistic talent made her bedroom come to life.

"Look up!" Izzie pointed at the stars, and she smacked off the lights, revealing they glowed in the dark along with the outline of the mermaid's tail.

"Wow."

Skylar hit the light switch and stood in the doorway. "It is something else," she said. "A bit too girly for my taste."

"Then I guess it's a good thing it isn't your bedroom." I probably should have held my tongue, but I was not too fond of the way Skylar spoke about Izzie, let alone behaved as if she couldn't understand. Isabella may have been three, but kids were smart. They picked up on everything.

"You ready for the tour?" Skylar picked at her nails, staring down at her hands.

"I'll be back," I said to Izzie and followed Skylar down the hall for the briefest tour possible. She opened Jaxson's door to his bedroom. "Dresser is in the corner. The bathroom door is next to it. I'll grab you a towel."

"Thank you."

She brushed past me and knocked into my shoulder. I bit back a yelp of pain.

The woman didn't know what I'd been through, and I wasn't about to confide in her.

She hated me. I wasn't sure why.

Was it because I slept with Jaxson? Did she know? Why did she care?

The bedroom dark, I flipped on the light, and a warm ambient glow cast from the ceiling fan and light overhead.

His king-sized mattress was pressed against the wall near the window, the bed made, the comforter perfectly centered with the pillows fluffed. I wanted to lie down, curl up under the sheets, but I couldn't invite myself into his bed.

He'd offered for me to stay at his house, not in his bedroom.

My teeth tugged on my bottom lip. Why had Jaxson run off without so much as a goodbye last night?

No note. No phone call or text. I couldn't think about that right now.

My eyelids drooped, exhausted from the day's events.

I tugged on the dresser's handle, the oak, heavy, robust. The rails glided open, and the top drawer revealed to me his boxers and socks.

This felt far too intimate after one night together that hadn't resulted in even waking up alongside one another. I slammed the drawer and tried the second one down, grabbing a dark red university t-shirt with the words *Montana Grizzlies*.

With my fist tight on the shirt, I brought it to my face. The soft material caressed my cheek as I drank in *his* scent. Although his room smelled uniquely of him, the t-shirt was muskier, stronger, and I clung to it.

Skylar strolled down the hall, and with the sound of her footsteps approaching, I lowered the soft tee.

She threw a fluffy mint bath towel at me.

"Thanks." I seized the linen, surprised she didn't bring me a hand towel or washcloth instead and tell me that's all there was clean.

With the softness of the towel in my palm, my grip tight on his tee, the dam nearly broke. No one would see my downfall, certainly not a girl I hadn't spent over five minutes with who wanted nothing to do with me.

I yanked open a second drawer with two pairs of sweatpants and grabbed the ones on top before fleeing to the master bathroom. I flipped the light and slammed the door shut behind me.

My chest seized and clenched tight. It was like I was drowning, the air not finding its way fast enough inside my lungs.

I stripped down, my clothes in a pile, and stumbled to the bathtub. The room spun, my feet unsteady beneath me. The wall held me up, my back to it, my breathing long yet shallow, gasping for air.

Blinding dots peppered my vision. I reached my arm into the tub, pushed past the curtain, and started the shower.

The only thing that mattered was getting every speck of dirt and grime from those bastards off my body.

I rubbed at my arms, scrubbing with my hands outside of the tub. The water was tepid. I cranked it hotter.

I needed to erase everything, destroy the filth burned to my flesh.

With my palm up, I tested the water, pleased that it was hot. Steam covered the mirror, and I stepped into the tub. The shower rained down.

With white knuckles, I snatched the bar of soap, scrubbing it over my skin. I needed to rid myself of their filth. I repeatedly washed—the heat from the shower leaving a blush over my body.

It wasn't enough. The dirt wouldn't disappear. The steam in the bathroom clouded my vision as it swirled in the air. Smoke.

The soap skidded out of my grasp to the tub. I dove for the slippery bar, my knees embracing the tub, the scorching water pouring over my head, gliding down my back.

My hands trembled. Tears flooded and broke free, the shower mixed with my defeat slipping down the drain. I pulled my knees to my chest. The water pounded against me, hot rain against my body.

The smell of smoke wafted in with an icy gust. I shuddered and buried my face into my bent knees.

A cool rush of air caressed my skin, causing goosebumps to cover me under the spray of water. I felt a shadow, a body standing above me. The sobs racked my body.

"Freckles." While I could hear his voice, I didn't move.

The shower shut off and a warm, fluffy towel wrapped around my shoulders.

I turned my head slightly to see him, to acknowledge he was real, and I wasn't hallucinating.

"Let's get you out of the shower," he whispered. His strong voice echoed in the bathroom but didn't pull me from being locked up inside my head. "The water is freezing."

I hadn't noticed when the temperature grew cool. My teeth chattered.

Drained of energy, I couldn't speak. I had no ability to move other than the tremors that I had no control over.

Tears wept from my soul and slid down my cheeks. The warm towel no longer offered as much comfort as the heat from the shower dissipated.

Jaxson scooped me up and lifted me into his arms.

I wanted to wrap my arms around his neck but that required more strength than I had in me. My eyelids drooped as I rested my wet head against his shirt.

He smelled of smoke and it tickled my nose as I breathed in his scent.

"I need to dry you off."

He held me tight in his embrace and gently guided me to stand in front of him, my feet on the warm, shaggy bath rug. I stared at the maroon which matched the color of my skin. Bruised, battered, beaten.

His touch was light and gentle, and he steadied me as I swayed. One hand remained planted on my hip, the other drying me off with the mint-colored towel.

I wanted to ask why he had green towels and red rugs. It felt odd but the words didn't reach my lips. I was stuck inside my head.

Each stroke of the towel and I swayed. "Okay, we're almost done. I'm going to put this on you and then tuck you into bed," Jaxson said, explaining everything he did.

He sat at the edge of the toilet and brought me closer. Each step I took seemed to take minutes in my head, tunnel vision, a nasty side effect I'd experienced time and time again.

Nudging me closer to the toilet, his legs straddled me, keeping me upright while he guided his university t-shirt over my arms and head, letting it fall around my waist. "I think pants are too much for you right now." He stared at me.

What was he thinking?

Was he repulsed by my inability to do anything but collapse?

CHAPTER TWENTY-SIX

JAXSON

I lifted Ariella into my arms and carried her from the bathroom to my bed. With a gentle finesse, I laid her down on the mattress and helped guide her under the warm downy blankets.

"Freckles?" My stomach clenched, concern in my tone. "Are you all right?"

She wasn't all right. Only an idiot would have asked such a stupid question.

I climbed atop the covers. My body nestled tight beside hers. She lay calm, motionless on her back, cocooned under the comforter and bedsheets.

I breathed in her scent and shut my eyes, smiling and torn up inside.

How was I going to handle letting her live under my roof but keeping things platonic? I never intended for last night to be a one-night stand but if we couldn't be together—I didn't want to finish that thought.

I kissed her cheek and stood.

Quiet as a mouse, I slipped out of the bedroom, grabbed a towel from the linen closet and hurried back to avoid Skylar.

I didn't want to deal with her tonight. I didn't have it in me to answer her questions or see the disapproving look cross her face.

I withdrew my phone from my pocket. A group text popped up for me on the main screen.

My vision glazed over the display, the letters blurring together. I'd read it later.

I stripped down and tossed my filthy clothes into the hamper. Doing my best to keep the noise down, I meandered into the bathroom and left the door slightly ajar. If she needed me, I wanted to hear her. I started the shower and was pleased the water had heated again.

Scrubbing the smoke, blood, and dried remnants of grime down the drain, I let the water immerse me as if nothing else existed.

One hand rested against the cold tile as water pounded my face, my chest, soaking me inside and out. My eyes burned and I shoved my face back under the hot spray. I rubbed my eyes and finished my shower.

When I was done, I slipped on a pair of boxers and sat at the edge of the mattress and reached for my phone.

I wouldn't be able to sleep without knowing what was sent.

Lincoln had sent a new text: *If you can keep it in your pants, she's hired. No fraternizing with the subordinate.*

The text had been sent to all of Eagle Tactical. Obviously, the guys had discussed hiring her. I assumed Mason had been behind it after our discussion in the truck earlier.

Relief should have washed over me, but it didn't.

Conflicted, hurt, the desire pent up inside of me would have to be squashed. We had to keep things platonic.

They were right, it would be for the best. If she would be living under my roof, we couldn't start a relationship and work together, not if I was her boss.

This was about *her*. What was in her best interest. Ariella came first.

I climbed under the covers beside her. It would be the last night we could share a bed.

Tomorrow, I would have to show her to the guest room, but tonight, I would savor the warmth of her body and the sweet smell of her scent on my pillow.

When I wrapped an arm around her waist, Ariella didn't stir. She was serene in slumber and I hoped her dreams offered her peace.

———

"Daddy!" Izzie's squeal brought me out of dreamland.

Sunlight poured in through the curtains. I buried my face in the pillow. Dawn broke. I wasn't ready to face the day, but my little munchkin made sure I was made aware of the hour.

I rubbed the sleep from my eyes and realized Ariella lay asleep beside me in bed. I held up my finger to my lips to indicate to Isabella to be quiet.

Climbing out of bed, the cold floor caused a shiver to run down my spine.

Izzie's eyes were wide and bright. I followed her out of the bedroom and closed the door, holding one hand on the wood to keep it from banging shut, steadying it.

She grasped onto my hand and I lifted my little munchkin into my arms, carrying her down the stairs.

"Breakfast?"

"Yes, I will make you breakfast," I rasped.

I tried to keep quiet not to wake Skylar, either.

When did she plan on leaving?

Izzie squirmed out of my arms and I sat her on the counter. "Pancakes, Daddy?"

Opening the pantry, I pulled out the pancake mix along with a bowl. "Yes, I can make pancakes for you this morning." I kissed her cheek.

Soft footsteps trampled down the back stairs. If I knew Skylar, she would sleep all afternoon. While she'd been up early yesterday to help with Izzie, if she didn't have to, she wouldn't.

"Good morning," Ariella's soft voice greeted. It was music to my ears.

I could get used to this, but things had to change. "Morning," I said. My tone came out gruffer than I intended.

She quirked an eyebrow and I offered her a smile, not wanting to alarm her.

"You look better."

Her gaze fell to the floor, a blush spread across her cheeks. Ariella nibbled on her bottom lip, avoiding my stare.

I wanted to reach out and guide her chin up to see her stare.

The guys were right, I had to keep things platonic between us. "I have some good news. Do you want to take a seat?"

She perched herself on the stool at the counter, seated near Izzie. She emitted a soft sigh before meeting my gaze.

I measured the pancake mix, pouring it into the bowl and then measured out the water.

"Sure," she said, making herself comfortable. When I didn't press about last night and her curled up in the shower, she seemed to relax.

Yanking the drawer open, I fished out a spoon and placed it on the counter. "I spoke with the guys last night." I had technically spoken with Mason, and Lincoln had responded on behalf of the team, but I didn't feel the need to elaborate.

"Oh?" She wiped her palms on her bare legs.

My tee shirt swept down to her knees much like a nightgown. She swam in my shirt and realizing there were no panties underneath made my heart race.

The kitchen seemed warmer than usual. I had Ariella to thank for that; my body responded to her sexiness and all she did was sit there innocently on the stool, listening to me.

"Yes. We'd like to invite you to work for Eagle Tactical," I said.

Ariella's eyes lit up. "Really?"

"Yes."

Isabella snatched the spoon from my grasp before I could stir the ingredients. She wanted to help.

"There are a few things we need to discuss, though, regarding your employment."

I let Izzie keep the spoon and pushed the bowl toward her. If she wanted to help, so be it. I could use all the help I could get, my stomach tensed.

My heart wouldn't stop pounding against my ribcage. Is that what Ariella felt every single day?

Her tongue swiped her top lip, and she rolled her lips tight between her mouth. "Yes?" The softest, most timid sound came from her mouth. Ariella sounded angelic and while I recognized that she had been with the C.I.A., I also understood she wasn't a field agent. Her responsibility with our team would be in the office, where she would be safe.

"I would like you to stay here, under my roof, at least until you get things settled." I didn't want her thinking that I was kicking her out or making her feel unwelcome with what I had to say next.

Her gaze went from me to Izzie. "Okay." After a beat, she glanced back at me. "Is that it?"

I wished that was all I had to say, but the guys were right. In order to protect Ariella, I had to put her first. "We need to keep things platonic between us. I'll be your boss at Eagle Tactical."

A rush of air expelled from her lips. Her face went ghostly pale. "Oh." She smiled, her lips tight, her eyes narrow. "Of course. That's fine. I wouldn't expect special treatment. It wouldn't be fair to your other employees."

She pushed herself off the stool and ran a hand through her unkempt hair.

"I should probably find something to wear. It's not appropriate for me to only be wearing a tee in front of my boss."

I didn't mind it, in fact I liked it a lot, but I had to let her go. "Feel free to borrow whatever you need from my dresser. We can go into town later today and go shopping for new clothes."

She rubbed her eyes.

I prayed she wasn't about to cry.

Shuffling her feet, she pointed behind herself at the stairs where she'd come down from minutes earlier. "I'll grab something from your dresser and then get out of your hair."

Ariella spun around to run away from me, but I wouldn't have it.

I stepped away from the counter and grabbed her by the waist. Turning her around to face me, one hand poised on her hip, the other in her hair.

I wanted to kiss her, to pull her body tight against mine and slide my knee between her thighs. Staring into her eyes, our breathing matched, heavy and deep.

"I thought we were going to keep things professional?" Ariella whispered, breathless.

I hated the guys. How easily I let them come between the woman I yearned for and my job. They were doing this to protect all of us, but why did it feel like hell?

Why did I have to choose? I could have both, just not in the way I desired.

Need poured through me, overtook every ounce of power inside of me.

I leaned down, demanding one last taste, a kiss, a rough fuck if she let me have her.

Ariella guided a hand to my chest. My heart pounded against her palm. "We can't do this. I need the job, I want to work for Eagle Tactical," she said, staring up at me with those powerful olive eyes. "It's a dream come true."

I wanted to be part of her dreams, the dirty kind that involved having my way with her on my desk. "You're always the sensible one," I said, unable to break my gaze away from her.

Somewhere between finding her on the road and saving her life, I'd fallen for her, hard.

EPILOGUE

Hazel

Had I known what this morning would bring, I would have run.

"Come with me." Nikolai yanked me by the arm, his grip marking my skin, leaving behind a lasting bruise.

"No." I shrugged out of his grasp. "Get off me. I'm not going anywhere with you." Just because we were bound by blood didn't mean I had to abide by *his* rules.

Nikolai Agron, the head of the Russian mob, was my jerk of a stepbrother.

"The deal has already been made. He'll take care of you and you'll give him children."

"I'm not marrying anyone because you arranged it." What century did he think we lived in? Had he lost his mind?

"You will do as you're told, Hazel." The way he said my name sent a shiver down my spine.

He towered above me and gripped my hair. Yanking my long curls, he brought my face to his. "You will marry Franco Ivanov and you will obey him."

I scoffed at his idea of marriage and the moment he loosened his grip on my hair, I spat in his face. "I'm not yours to give away or sell." He backhanded me across the face.

"I own you! Don't you ever forget that, little sister."

———

Thank you for reading Expose: Jaxson!

I hope you love Ariella and Jaxson. Their story continues in STEALTH: MASON!

Sold to the mafia. I'm nothing more than a piece of property to my brother. Forced into an arranged marriage, I enlist the help of Eagle Tactical.

Ariella

I moved in with Jaxson after the attack. It's hard to keep my hands off him, but he's my boss. He's given me a job at Eagle Tactical as his subordinate.

I don't take orders well, especially from a grumpy boss. He's about as grumpy as his toddler when she skips her afternoon nap.

Jaxson

I vowed to protect Ariella. That's how much she means to me, but she's gotten under my skin with her know everything attitude and sassy hip sway that has my body in overdrive.

I swore I'd never do a one-night stand. Is that what she thinks we shared? Is that why she hates me?

I don't know how much longer I can wake up under the same roof, go to work with her, and not throw her down on the bed.

We have a mission that takes priority, but how can I keep my mind on the job when she's always in the room, and I want to bend her over the desk?

One-click STEALTH: MASON now!

And sign up for my newsletter to find out about new books, giveaways, and freebies: www.authorwillowfox.com/subscribe

I appreciate your help in spreading the word, including telling a friend. Reviews help readers find books! Please leave a review on your favorite book site.

GIVEAWAYS, FREE BOOKS, AND MORE GOODIES!

I hope you enjoyed EXPOSE and will continue the journey with Jaxson, Ariella, and the Eagle Tactical team.

While this is my first novel as Willow Fox, I've been published professionally since 2013.

Sign up for my Willow Fox newsletter

If you enjoyed EXPOSE, please take a moment to leave a review. Reviews helps other readers discover my books.

Not sure what to write? That's okay. It doesn't have to be long. You can share how you discovered my book; was it a recommendation by a friend or a book club?

Let readers know who your favorite character is or what you'd like to see happen next. Do you normally read HEA? How are you feeling about the HFN? (I hope satisfied but I promise I will be delivering a HEA at the end of the series!)

Thank you for reading! I hope you'll consider joining my mailing list for free books, promotions, giveaways, and new release news.

ABOUT THE AUTHOR

Willow Fox has loved writing since she was in high school (many ages ago). Her small town romances are reflective of living in a small town in rural America.

Whether she's writing romance or sitting outside by the bonfire reading a good book, Willow loves the magic of the written word.

She dreams of being swept off her feet and hopes to do that to her readers!

Visit her website at:

https://authorwillowfox.com

Jailed Little Jade

Prefer a sweeter romance with action and adventure?
Check out these titles under the name Ruth Silver.

Aberrant Series

Love Forbidden

Secrets Forbidden

Magic Forbidden

Escape Forbidden

Refuge Forbidden

Boxsets

Gem Apocalypse

Nightblood

Royal Reaper

Royal Deception

Standalones

Stolen Art

www.ingramcontent.com/pod-product-compliance
Lightning Source LLC
La Vergne TN
LVHW040321140725
816065LV00010B/270